CORK CITY LIBRAR

This book is due for return on the last date stamped below.
Overdue fines: 10c per week plus postage.

Class no. ....   Accn no. ....

SOMETHING
BEGINNING WITH

SOMETHING
BEGINNING WITH

SARAH SALWAY

BLOOMSBURY

First published in Great Britain in 2004

Extract taken from *Roland Barthes* by Roland Barthes,
Papermac 1989. Reproduced by permission of Palgrave Macmillan.

The moral right of the author has been asserted

Bloomsbury Publishing Plc, 38 Soho Square, London W1D 3HB

A CIP catalogue record for this book
is available from the British Library

ISBN 0 7475 6922 3

10 9 8 7 6 5 4 3 2 1

Typeset by Hewer Text Ltd, Edinburgh

All papers used by Bloomsbury Publishing are natural,
recyclable products made from wood grown in sustainable,
well-managed forests. The manufacturing processes conform
to the environmental regulations of the country of origin.

Printed in Great Britain by Clays Ltd, St Ives plc

For all the generous women I am lucky enough to call my friends, especially Kay, Annemarie, Debbie, Marnie, Lynne and Ali.
And for Alice, with respect.

The alphabetical order erases every-thing, banishes every origin. Perhaps in places, certain fragments seem to follow one another by some affinity; but the important thing is that these little networks not be connected, that they do not slide into a single enormous network which would be the structure of the book, its meaning. It is in order to halt, to deflect, to divide this descent of discourse toward a destiny of the subject, that at certain moments the alphabet calls you to order (to disorder) and says: Cut! Resume the story in another way.

Roland Barthes

A

Ambition

My best friend's nine-year-old cousin can't decide whether she wants to be an astronaut or Prime Minister. When I was young, I used to want to be either beautiful or a farmer's wife. I couldn't be both because if I was beautiful, then there was no way I would settle for just a farmer. I would be good enough for my very own sugar daddy. I knew what a sugar daddy was before I had heard of an engineer or a chartered surveyor.

See *Attitude, Bosses, Colin, Firefighting, Promotion, Ultimatum*

Ants

I was sitting in the park during my lunch hour when an ant crawled over my leg. I squashed it with my thumb and flicked off its body with my fingers. Then I carried on eating my sandwiches.

Ants have not always left me so cold. I must have been about eleven when I found an ant colony in our garden. You have never seen anything so marvellous. It was like watching algebra in action. The worker ants walked in straight lines everywhere and seemed to know exactly where they were going.

But then I remembered something I'd learnt at school and drew a line with my black felt-tip right across their path. It threw them into confusion. They wouldn't cross it even though it was just a drawing.

I told my father this at lunchtime. He said that we should respect ants for their innate civilisation. They even milked aphids, he said, in the same way we milk cows. He went on and on about how clever ants were in a way he never talked about me.

After lunch, I boiled a kettle and poured the hot water over the colony. I sat there and watched the ants die. My eyes hurt from where I squeezed them together to make the tears come.

At supper, neither my father nor I said anything to each other. I was worried he might ask me why.

See *Dogs, Engagement Ring, Jealousy, Outcast, Revenge, Tornados*

Attitude

I work as a secretary in the media. The company I work for specialises in writing and producing technical newsletters for small to medium-sized industrial businesses. Working in the media is something I don't always talk about because some people seem to think I'm showing off. This is something I would never do, but it's hard when all everybody wants to know is what it's like to have such an exciting job. Maybe this is why people in the media tend to stick together. But then again the strange thing I have noticed is when they're together, the only thing they talk about is what they are GOING to do – and not what they DO do. It seems they are all just filling in time before they become writers, or film directors, or actors, or painters. It makes me feel dull for enjoying my job because there is absolutely nothing else I can imagine myself doing.

See *Dreams, Impostor Syndrome, Wobbling*

B

Baked Beans

My grandmother on my mother's side was a young girl in Liverpool during the war. She can still remember the night the Heinz factory was bombed and how for days afterwards the city smelt of cooked baked beans. It made them even hungrier than they were already.

Her mother – my great-grandmother – once spotted an unexploded bomb caught in a tree near their house. For hours she ran round getting people out of their houses and down to the shelter, where my grandmother was hiding. My great-grandmother wheeled the sick down, helped mothers with little children and reassured the elderly.

She must have saved many, many lives that night so I can't blame my grandmother for still being annoyed, years later, that they didn't give her mother a medal for her bravery. Instead, they gave it to the lady who was in charge of making tea.

See *God, Mystery Tours, Noddy*

Best Friends

At the age of twenty-five, my best friend Sally has become the mistress of a millionaire called Colin. This is not something that normally happens in our town. Just in films. She has given up her job, her nights out with the girls and living in her studio flat. Because Colin has set her up in a flat near his office, she has taken a lodger to pay the mortgage on her own flat. And all this without a backward glance. Recently she spent five hours trying to find a dressmaker who was prepared to pick her jeans apart by hand and re-sew them so the tight seams would make no marks on her skin when Colin pulled them down. We are no longer such good friends. She says she can't bear the way I look at her these days.

See *Danger, Friends, Influences, Ultimatum, Yields, Zzzz*

Blackbirds, Robins and Nightingales

Sometimes it is hard to distinguish between how you sound in your head and how other people seem to hear you.

For instance, I have noticed that I can make what I think is a perfectly pleasant comment but that it can still cause offence. I do not mean to have a sharp tongue, it is just the way the words come out.

Perhaps it is because I have such low self-esteem and do not think so much of myself as someone like Sally, for instance.

Personally though, I blame the nuns. At the convent school I went to, we were split into three groups for singing. There were the Nightingales who could sing beautifully, the Blackbirds who were all right, and the Robins who were what Mother Superior called 'orally challenged'. I was one of only three Robins in the whole school, although I had a cold at the auditions so it wasn't really fair.

The Robins were hardly ever allowed to sing in public and particularly not if the song was anything to do with God. We had to mouth along instead, which got very boring, and sometimes it was hard to keep the words in. Once, an unidentified Robin joined in with an especially loud and lively hymn, one we all loved.

In the middle of our Lord stamping out the harvest, Mother Superior held out her hand for silence.

'Hark!' she said, raising her other hand to her ear. 'I can hear a Robin singing.' Everyone looked at me.

That moment has always stayed with me. One of the things I hate most about myself is the way I blush in public even though I am not necessarily to blame. It is the same feeling that makes you itch every time anyone talks about fleas.

See *Captains, God, Outcast, Voices*

Blood

It used to be a craze at school to scratch the initials of your boyfriend into your arm with a compass and squeeze the skin until the blood came up. Then you'd rub ink over the graze so you were tattooed for life. Luckily it rarely worked.

Once I was doing it with Sally, but as neither of us had a boyfriend at that time, we just dug the compass randomly into each other's arm. It made me think of the time I punctured my aunt's favourite leather sofa one Christmas with the screwdriver from the toy carpentry set I'd got from Santa. I did that again and again too.

It was Sally's idea to mix the blood drops together. She kept flicking her cigarette lighter and we sang 'Kumbaya' as we did it to make it seem more meaningful. Sally said that we were sisters now and that nothing could separate us, not even a boy.

See *Codes, Mars Bars, Vendetta, Yields, Zzzz*

Bosses

The only trouble with my job is the bosses. My current one is possibly the worst I have ever had. He is called Brian. He is from Yorkshire and has a short bristly beard which he is always fondling and if I don't manage to look away, I can sometimes see his little tongue hanging out, all red and glistening.

Brian won't leave me alone. He seems to think we have a special relationship. He's always telling me that I mustn't mind if he teases me, that he does it to everyone he's fond of. 'It means you're one of the family, Ver,' he says, putting his arm round me.

It's funny though that while Brian is always standing too close to me, when it comes to work he likes to dictate his typing for me into a machine, rather than face to face. He'll do it even if I'm in the room and he'll leave little messages to me which means I have to hear them twice. Once he said into the machine: 'Good morning, Verity, you're looking very nice this morning,' so I called across, 'Thank you, Brian,' and he told me off for spoiling his dictation. He said he'd have to start again now. I left the room and when I eventually listened to his tape I noticed that this time he didn't say I looked nice.

Another time he dictated a rude joke to me. A man in an office asked to borrow another man's Dictaphone. The other man said no, he couldn't. He should use his finger to dial like everyone else.

I listened to this through my headphones with a stony face because I knew Brian was watching me, hoping I would laugh.

See *Ambition, Zero*

Boxing

I didn't tell Brian that Sally and I had started going to a Boxercise class at the local sports centre. It would only have turned him on.

I wasn't very good at first. The instructor was American, a big man with a ponytail he was too old for. He followed me over to the punchbag and shouted out loudly that I was too much of a girl to box. He said it was because I was English and had been brought up to be polite. 'Who would you like that punchbag to be?' he asked. 'Who really pisses you off?'

I couldn't think of anyone. I wouldn't really want to hurt Brian, even. Anyway, I told the instructor that I was half Irish. On my mother's side. He said in that case I definitely had to hit it harder. Harder, harder, harder. Eventually, I swung at it so hard that I kept on spinning even though I'd thrown my punch. The instructor clapped me on the back then and called me champ. He even started to sing 'When Irish Eyes Are Smiling'.

Sally and I couldn't stop laughing afterwards. When we went for a drink, I noticed that we didn't hang back as we sometimes do at the bar. We made sure we got served straight away and then we took the best seats in the pub. When a man came to talk to us, Sally didn't flirt and throw her hair over her shoulder. She told him straight to go away. That she wanted to talk to her friend.

'You gave it hell, Verity,' she kept saying, toasting me with her beer. 'You gave it hell.'

The next day, I walked sharper, straighter. As if I wasn't a girl at all.

See *Gossip, Lesbians, Moustache, Weight*

Breasts

Last week I was on my way home from work, walking past the wine bar, when a handsome Australian stopped me. He was dressed in a business suit, aged about thirty, very tanned, broad. He asked whether I'd have a drink with him. He said he was only in town for a couple of days, didn't know London well, and was lonely. I weighed up my options – drinks and a few laughs with him versus a microwaved meal in front of *EastEnders*.

When he ordered the bottle of wine, however, he asked

for three glasses. Then his friend joined us. He was Australian too, but not tanned, not broad, aged around fifty. I didn't know you could get boring Aussies with glasses, hairy ears and skinny bodies, but you can.

They talked together a lot of the time about inter-computer networking, html, broadband versus bluewave, although every so often Peter, the young one, would look at me and wink. I suppose he meant to include me but I was beginning to wonder why I was there. Then Peter went to the toilet, and after we'd sat there in silence for a bit, the other man leant across the table and asked me how much. His breath smelt of pear drops, I remember, and all the time I was thinking how much what? How much wine? How much time?

And then I realised.

I was running down the street, my face red, when Peter caught up with me. He grabbed my arm. I was shouting no, no, but weakly, so he turned me towards him and we kissed then. You know how sometimes when you kiss someone your tongues intertwine and you feel what's like an electric shock racing through your body. As if your kiss has connected two wires between you but all the resulting fizzles, crackles and sparks are going on between your legs, not in your mouth. That's what happened then. That's why I agreed to go back to his hotel with him.

He touched my breasts a lot.

It is something I am sensitive about. You see, my breasts are very big. People can sometimes be cruel and shout out things about them in the street. I hated them when I was growing up. I used to wear a too-tight swimming costume under my clothes to hold them down so no one would notice them. It used to make going to the toilet exhausting because I'd have to take everything off. Plus at school we used to have these very short doors in the ladies so I had to hold up all my clothes at waist height with one hand so no one could see.

Of course, I wasn't a virgin when I made love to Peter, but it was the first time anyone had touched my breasts like that. As if they weren't dirty, weren't something to be ashamed about. It seemed to mean something.

We had breakfast together in the morning and he kissed me goodbye. There in the restaurant, like we were a proper married couple or something.

When I got into work, I didn't tell anyone. People kept saying how quiet I was. I went to the loo after a bit, and when I pulled down my knickers I could smell Peter. That's when I started to cry.

I haven't heard from him since. It was my first time with a stranger like that. I hope it will be my last. I thought Colin was going to be a one-night stand for Sally at first. I get angry with Sally sometimes that she doesn't seem to feel the same guilt I felt about Peter.

See *Colin, True Romance*

C

Captains

This is how Sally and I first became friends.

Like the singing, in my head I am completely co-ordinated as far as sports are concerned. Now I am an adult I don't have to do anything I don't want to, but I still like to lie in bed imagining how I can catch ball after ball in hands that open and caress rather than sting painfully. My legs find such a sweet rhythm as I run the 800 metres that I almost levitate off the ground, able to go on and on and on as I race past all the other runners.

In reality, I became the school expert at the rain-dance I created in the hope that games would be cancelled. It wasn't just the humiliation, it was the way your legs would get so cold on the hockey pitch, the skin red and blue and sharp with pain.

Sally walked in once just as I was jumping up and down in the deserted shower rooms, hands on top of my head, elbows flapping. I was chanting 'Whoah, whoah, whoah, rain, rain, rain.'

She took one look and left. I thought she might have been smiling but I'd been too embarrassed to look closely. Neither of us said anything.

An hour later we were standing at the edge of the sports field in the perfect sunshine. Sally was at the front by the games teacher as she was always one of the team captains. I was standing at the back so I wouldn't have to keep getting out of the way when the other, more popular, girls were picked for the teams.

I thought it was a joke when Sally chose me before anyone else. I didn't want to go up at first but everyone kept prodding me. Sally always picked me first after that.

I never asked her why, even afterwards when we took a vow to tell each other everything. I always hoped it was because Sally was the one person who could look into my head and see those sweet catches I made in my dreams. How perfect everything was there.

See *Blackbirds, Robins and Nightingales, Kindness, Vendetta, X-ray Vision*

Codes

S all yan dI u se dt owrit eletter si ncod ebu twhe nyo utak ei ta sseriousl ya stha tyo uhav et ohav esomethin gt osa y. N othin gi swors etha ngoin gt oth etroubl eo funcoverin ga s ecre tan dfindin gnothin gther e. T hat' swhe nw estarte dshopliftin g. W e' dwrit elist so fwha twe' dtake ni nou rcod e. I t hin ktha twa swh yw ewer eneve rcaugh t. I

14

fpeopl ecan' tunderstan dyo u, t he yten dt omak eyo
uinvisibl e. T he ydon' tbothe rwit hyo u.

See *Friends, Indecent Exposure, Woolworth's, Yields, Zzzz*

Colin

I am starting to get suspicious about Colin. Maybe it's a
hangover after my escapade with Peter, but I worry about
the way he seems to treat Sally so casually.

Sally says that as long as he pays the bills and keeps her
happy, she doesn't mind if he is the mad axe-man. She
says his attitude is a relief.

'I'm blossoming,' she says, and so she is.

I try to be happy for her but when I walk up and down
the road where Sally says Colin lives with his wife and
family, I see no sign of him. I can't smell Colin in the air.
Also, he is spending more and more time with Sally in
what she calls their 'love nest'.

'Isn't his wife jealous?' I ask.

'If Colin doesn't mind, who cares?' Sally says, and I
must admit it seems a little bit odd that it's me who does.

See *Best Friends, Foreheads, Love Calculators, Stalking,
Youth*

Crème Caramel

Sally has a friend who can suck up a whole crème caramel
from a plate in one go. I have seen her do it. She stands
over the table, with her hands behind her back, and then

she hoovers it up in one go without leaving a drop either on the plate or round her lips.

Sally herself can fit thirty-eight Maltesers into her mouth at once. She has to stuff them round her lips and in the spaces at the back of her jaw. It is not a very attractive trick, especially when she has to spit them all out again. But then neither is the crème caramel sucking-up, but at parties, people always ask to see them. It makes Sally and her friend the centre of attention, and the rest of us feel jealous.

Unfortunately I don't like either Maltesers or crème caramel and the one trick I do know is very complicated, involving three packs of cards. Could this be where I am going wrong?

See *Captains, Underwear, Wobbling*

D

Daisies

My mother told me once that I was not sweet enough to be called after a flower. Something useful, yes, but not a flower. Her name was Rose and I thought if I also had a pretty name then I'd look more like her.

I called myself Daisy in secret and would talk about myself in the third person. 'Daisy's nearly ready for bed now,' or 'Look how pretty Daisy looks in the mirror.' It made me feel like I belonged. But then one day I blurted out something about wanting to be called Daisy and everyone laughed.

'It sounds more like a cow,' said my father, and he smiled fondly at my mother.

See *Ants, Names, True Romance, Zest*

Danger

Sally will always be my only real friend although I hope she never finds that out. She would probably think it was funny.

When we were growing up, our families were very different. Her parents used to go to the pub and drink sweet liqueurs which made her mother giggle. They were also what my parents called 'Sunday drivers', which meant they went on outings. If I was lucky, they'd take me with them sometimes. Sally's mother called us 'the girls', which I liked because it made me seem like a second daughter. As if Sally and I were interchangeable.

Once, we all went to a fête in the country and watched a local girl being crowned the Rose Queen. She sat giggling on a throne, holding a bunch of roses and surrounded by Rose Princes. These princes were all spotty and fat. The dishy boys were too busy throwing grass over the Rose Princesses to look at the Queen. The minute they'd put the crown on her, she'd become too much for them although we couldn't see why she'd been picked in the first place.

Sally and I soon got bored because no one was throwing grass over us, so we went to look round. We found a bridge that was very crowded so we joined the throng going over it. When we reached the middle, we suddenly heard the cracking and splitting of wood and the bridge gave way.

Later, the man who owned the house and gardens came out and said that the trouble was that the bridge didn't lead anywhere, just to a shut gate, so what had happened was that people were coming straight back at the same time as others were crossing and that meant there was too much weight in the middle for the bridge to hold. Considering the danger we'd all come through, he was surprisingly unsympathetic. It was the last time he was holding the fête in his grounds, he said, because he didn't understand why the public were all so keen to go over a bridge that went nowhere. And now he'd have to have the bridge mended, which was going to cost money he didn't have.

I read about an experiment which made men go over a very dangerous bridge and when they got to the other side they were shown photographs of women. All the men found the women more attractive than they would have done if they had not had such an exciting experience. However, Sally and I both agreed that when the Rose Queen came to wish us well in the Red Cross Tent she was so ugly, we still wondered why she had been crowned.

Sally has always taken me places, shown me the way to behave, what to do. Sometimes I wonder if this is why she likes me. Sometimes I wonder if where she takes me is always the best place to go.

See *Best Friends, Worst Case Scenario*

Dogs

The chairman of our company has a Dalmatian dog called Jupiter. When he brings it into work, we have to take it in turns to walk it at lunchtime. He seems to think it is a treat for us, and makes jokes about how many girlfriends his dog has. It does make you wonder what he thinks we are.

Susan, the receptionist, once told me that she had taken a call from his French au pair. This girl was in tears because she had broken the vacuum cleaner when she was outside, hoovering the lawn. Susan told her to take the vacuum cleaner inside and pretend it had never happened, but the girl kept crying, saying how much trouble she'd get into if the Chairman's wife came back and found anything left on the grass.

Perhaps the wife was getting her revenge. You are always hearing stories about au pairs getting off with their bosses. The Chairman is good-looking enough. I have often smiled at him on the stairs or when we meet in the office, but I'm not sure he even notices me. He always calls me Veronica and laughs in this coughing little way when he sees me.

I remember reading that a jilted girlfriend once got her own back on her boyfriend by letting herself into his flat when he was away and planting grass seed all over the carpet. She went in every morning of his holiday and watered it. I would have loved to have seen his face when he opened the door.

We never had a dog, although I wanted one. I used to imagine waking up nearly every morning and hearing one barking for me downstairs. Once I picked a particularly beautiful leaf and kept it in a glass bowl as a pet until I got bored of it. I do realise how pathetic this may sound now, but at the time I really loved that leaf.

See *Ambition, Revenge, Tornados*

Doors

It is impossible to have an advertisement in Britain which features a shut door. This is because so many children were locked in their bedrooms that even as adults, they automatically start to panic when the door isn't open. Even just an inch.

There were times when my mother used to tell me to stay in my bedroom. It wasn't cruel, she just wanted a break from looking after me. I'd have as many books as I wanted, treats to eat. I'd make myself a nest up there.

I always came down when my father came home though. I was so happy to see him, but he'd be tired after his day at work. He said he just wanted to spend some quiet time with my mother. I had so much to talk about, after my day reading, but he didn't seem to want to hear it.

See *Houses, Noddy, Property, Velvet, Yellow*

Dreams

Sally once went out with a man who liked to record her dreams in a diary. She had to break off with him because she got too exhausted. She'd be awake all night trying to think of interesting things for him to write about.

See *Codes, Mistaken Identity, Utopia*

E

Ears

I like to stick cotton-wool buds in my ears and turn them round, pushing harder and harder. I crave the satisfaction it brings. Sometimes when friends are round, all I can think of is that round plastic jar of baby buds until I have to go into my bedroom and clean my ears. It's like an itch. Once I twisted too hard and my head filled with a howling pain. I vowed then never to do it again, until the next time.

There was a boy at school called Stewart Griffiths. One day he was swinging on his chair during Geography when the teacher called him to attention and as he fell, the compass he was nudging at his ear pierced right through his eardrum. He screamed.

Three years later, when I joined the class, the other children were still talking about the loudness of that scream. When we were fifteen, I went out with Stewart Griffiths and felt the reflected glory from his fame. He would still scream in the playground for money.

The trouble was that Stewart was boring when he wasn't making a noise. He wanted to be a lorry driver and sometimes when we were lying together on his bed, he'd be able to name the type of lorry that went past the window just from the sound of its tyres. He seemed to feel this was particularly clever as he was still deaf in one ear from the compass incident.

See *Captains, The Fens, Sounds*

Elephant's Egg

We went to London Zoo for my eighth birthday and I fell in love with the elephants. I wanted to move in with them and be the little elephant that never strayed from her mother's side. I wanted people to say how sweet I was, and take pictures of me, and have my father wrap his trunk around me, swishing the flies off or sprinkling water over me to wash my back.

The following year, the day before my birthday, I asked to go and see the elephants again. My mother got cross and said money didn't grow on trees, but when I got back from school that afternoon, there was a message from the Zoo. Apparently, the elephant at London Zoo had laid an egg especially for me and my family to eat. It was going to come on my birthday.

The only trouble was that the zookeeper left it on our doorstep during the only two minutes in the day that I stopped watching for him. I took it into the kitchen where my mother was waiting to cook it. She was cross with me for not keeping a proper look-out because it meant she couldn't thank the keeper for bringing it all that way.

This happened every year until I was fifteen. I never managed to catch the zookeeper. My mother never managed to thank him.

An elephant's egg is not like an ordinary egg. The white tastes like mashed potato, and the yolk is never runny, being a bit like a large round sausage. I've had sausage and mashed potatoes many times since, but never anything as good as those elephant's eggs.

See *The Queen, The Queen II*

Endings

Ever since the Australian incident, I have been spending more time in my flat. My best treat is to pop into a bookshop and pick up a book to read. Then I curl up on the sofa with a bottle of wine and read myself into a trance.

The sort of books I like best are those in which I can completely lose myself. At first, you sit with the unopened book on your lap waiting to meet the main character with that sense of anticipation you get on blind dates. Is this person going to be your new best friend? And then there's a moment – normally just over half-way through – when your heart grows until it's too big for your body because all these dreadful things are happening in the book and there's nothing you can do to stop it. You can't even tell the character they're making all the wrong decisions. You've just got to keep on reading. But then you get to the last words and you can't believe it, you keep your fingers on the end sentence because it can't all finish there. It's as if they've shut the door and left you on the other side, unwanted. And you cared so much. And there's no way to make them see how much you cared.

A teacher at school told us that fairy stories always end with the prince and princess living happily ever after because what the writers were really saying, but couldn't, was that they would die eventually. Apparently it's a way of helping children to understand life and death. It was raining when he was telling us this. I'll never forget the sound of the rain falling on the flat roof of the classroom. Somehow it always rained when he read us stories that year.

Anyway, what he told us, very sternly, was that no one could expect to live happily ever after. It just didn't happen. There are no happy endings, he said.

See *Breasts, Stepmothers, True Romance, Yellow, Zzzz*

Engagement Ring

Colin has given Sally a ring. It isn't an engagement ring, but that's the finger she wears it on even though I tell her it's bad luck.

She won't let me try it on or even touch it. She says she remembers me telling her about how I posted my mother's engagement ring into my piggy bank when I was six.

It's true my mother cried in secret for days after the ring first went missing. She didn't tell anyone. That was the strange thing. She didn't even tell my father. I'm sure about this because I think if she had, he'd have started one of those inquisitions he was so fond of. Instead, she was quieter than normal. I'd come across her in odd rooms, frantically searching through cupboards, drawers, pockets, piles of things. Sometimes her eyes looked white and strained as if she was forcing herself not to weep.

Sally still can't understand why I never told my mother what I had done, but it was one of those china piggy banks you had to break to open and I loved the spotty smoothness of my pig. And then, of course, I left it too late. I wouldn't have been able to put the ring back on the dressing table and pretend it hadn't happened because Mum had moved the table to the other side of the room. I guess now she'd been taking up the carpet to check the ring hadn't fallen down there.

Dad went mad when he found my mother had lost her ring, but it was such a long time afterwards that I couldn't feel guilty any more. If my mother had really cared she'd have made a fuss at the time. She was always losing things.

See *Daisies, Mistaken Identity, True Romance, Voices*

F

Fashion

My favourite book when I was growing up was called *The Little White Horse*. There were two things about it I remember particularly. One was the sugary biscuits that were left in a silver tin in the heroine's tower bedroom. Some even had little pastel flowers iced on them. The other was the heroine's journey to the castle to stay with her unknown uncle. She was nervous, but still able to get pleasure from her beautiful laced-up boots tucked away under her long skirts. Even though no one else could see them, she knew they were there and that was enough.

It gave me a thrill of recognition. It probably shaped my life. Made me see the strength you could get from having the right kind of secrets.

I spend a lot of time shopping. I search out clothes which have special things about them only I will know about. I hug these to me. A certain colour that makes you want to eat it; a lining of soft plum silk; the Liberty print trim to a denim pocket; a perfectly shaped pleat which kicks up the edge of a skirt.

Coco Chanel knew all about this. She used to sew a gold chain invisibly into the hems of her jackets so they would be ideally weighted around the bottom.

I think if I could have a jacket like that I would die happy. I'd be buried in it.

See *Codes, Underwear, Women's Laughter*

Fat Women

I am the last person to judge anyone else based on appearances alone, but have you noticed how difficult it is to see a fat woman and a small thin man together and not think of them having violent, needy and possibly perverted sex?

See *Indecent Exposure, Sex, Toys, Voyeur, Weight, Wrists*

The Fens

Every time I tell people I come from the Fens, the only thing they can think of to say is, 'Well, there's certainly a lot of sky there.' If this is the first thing you think of, here are three things you might not know about the Fens:

1. A lot of the children I went to school with had webbed feet. In the Fens, this is quite usual. They weren't heavy like duck feet, but just a sliver of thin skin, so transparent as to be like silver, between each toe and the

next. When these children flexed their toes, it was the most beautiful sight you could imagine, especially after swimming when the drops of water would glisten and sparkle.

2.   The roads in the Fens are long and straight and run alongside treacherous dykes. They look even straighter because the houses on either side are slipping lower and lower back into the soil. If you are quiet you can almost hear it sucking at you. Anyway, because it gets so dark at night – all that sky – a lot of people have accidents and drive into the ditches and die. Often when you are driving in the Fens during the daylight, you see bouquets of flowers by the side of the road from the night before.

At the bank opposite our house, a doctor had a terrible accident with his wife. He managed to get out of the car before it got submerged but she drowned. He was so grief-stricken that he sat on the side until he was sure she had died. It became a craze for many months afterwards, imagining just what it must have felt like with all that water pressing against the car window, and being able to see your husband through the waves, watching you scream.

3.   Not many people appreciate that if you lie in a field of broad bean plants in flower, just as the sun is going down, you will find yourself surrounded by the smell of Chanel No. 5. It just goes to show that if you know where to look there is beauty in even the most unlikely places.

See *Fat Women*

Firefighting

Sometimes when I'm busy at work, I think of Sally's new life and wonder how she is keeping herself occupied. When we left school and started work, we had so many plans. We were going to start a business together and although we could never decide what to do we had lots of ideas. We were going to train in martial arts and hire ourselves out as bodyguards. We'd look like classy dates, but if someone tried to kill our partners, we'd be able to high-kick our way out of trouble. We were going to run a truly caring removal company, make novelty cushions, revamp people's wardrobes. In the meantime, I went to work for a bank and Sally got a job selling advertising space for the local newspaper. That's when she persuaded me to follow her into the media, although I was worried at first because my personality has never been as bouncy as hers. I could never cold-call like Sally could.

For example, one summer holiday Sally got us both a job selling fire extinguishers. We were supposed to walk into shops and while one of us distracted the shop assistant, the other would start a small fire which we would then put out with the fire extinguisher to show how efficient it was.

My father found out what we had to do on the day we were supposed to start, and banned me from joining Sally on safety grounds, and although she kept telling me what fun she was having and how much I was missing out, I was secretly relieved. Sometimes the things Sally makes herself do frighten me.

See *Attitude, Danger, Impostor Syndrome, Sex*

Foreheads

Sally asked me what I thought of Colin.

I said he was OK. Nothing special. Nothing worth throwing your life away for. But then Sally said that Colin had told her I was a bit intense. Apparently I keep staring at him.

At first I didn't know what he was talking about. But then I realised. Colin plays rugby. He'd come to the pub with a group of his friends after they'd been playing in the park. It's true, I couldn't stop looking at them. They all had the same foreheads. A bulging shelf that hung over their eyes and made them look unfocused and brainless. Other men didn't have this. They even shared the same wavy wrinkles across their foreheads. It was as if an empty space had been badly filled with cement and then someone had made patterns on it with a comb when it was still wet.

I wanted to ask why rugby players look and sound permanently concussed, but they were all too busy talking to each other and ignoring Sally and me. I didn't think Colin had seen me looking.

See *Nostrils, Vendetta, X-rated, Youth*

Friends

Every time I go out now with the girls we talk about Sally.

I think that nowadays we spend more time thinking about her than we ever did when she was spending time with us. We wonder if she's really happy, if she thinks Colin is genuine in his desire for her, what it must be like to have such a one-sided relationship. We agree we only have her best interests at heart.

We are supportive even though Sally doesn't always deserve it. I know that Miranda hasn't forgotten the time we were talking about making love and she was explaining the importance of truly caring for the other person and treating yourself as if you were someone precious.

'I could never have inappropriate meaningless sex,' Miranda said. She was so earnest that Sally was the only one round the table who didn't nod.

'I could,' she said, staring at the businessman on the next table and ignoring Miranda's frown. She left the restaurant with the businessman, and afterwards she wouldn't tell anyone what happened. Not even when we begged. She said we wouldn't approve.

It was so typical of her, but even so, the last thing we all want is for Sally's relationship not to work out.

Whenever I ring Sally to pass on everyone's best wishes, she laughs.

'We're here waiting for you if things don't work out,' I tell her and she says that's just what she's worried about.

See *Outcast, Vendetta*

G

Glenda G-Spot

I told Monica at work that I didn't go out very much in the evening so she invited me around to her house. I thought it was just going to be the two of us, but when I got there I found she was having a sex party.

This is like Tupperware for desperate women although we didn't do 'it', in fact not much of the evening was about actually doing 'it'. There were just lots and lots of gadgets for sale which simulated doing 'it'. There were about ten women there, all older than me. Monica's age. We sat in a circle and passed these gadgets round, sometimes without saying a word. Every so often Monica walked round with a tray of little biscuits smeared with houmous and pâté and filled up our glasses with fizzy sweet wine.

The woman who was organising the party was like a perverted Mary Poppins. Just when you thought it was all finished, she put her hand into an enormous canvas bag and pulled out something else. She made us play games and gave us all silly names. I was Glenda G-Spot, Monica was Wendy Wetdream and the girl sitting next to me was Cathy Come. It was hard to know whether to call each other by our real names or the names on the labels the woman stuck on our chests.

Cathy Come and I got into the final of one game where we had to pass an enormous black dildo under our chins between one another without dropping it. Cathy Come cheated because she kept angling it so it was difficult to get hold of. Mind you, I was quite pleased to come second because Cathy won the dildo but I got a bottle of an apricot-flavoured sauce which seemed nicer somehow.

I left when the woman drew out a blow-up man from her bag. One of his legs was stapled up from when a dog had got hold of it, she said. The air kept fizzling out of him, and I don't like to say where the nozzle was to blow into.

See *Liqueur Chocolates, Names, Toys*

Glitter

It worries me that all everyone thinks about these days is sex. I asked Sally about this and she told me a story the other day about a friend of hers who is a nurse. This friend's elderly mother came to stay the night before she was due to have a gynaecological examination in the hospital Sally's friend works in. The mother was very nervous so she spent a lot of time preparing in Sally's friend's bathroom before her appointment. She wanted to be very clean because no man had looked at her 'down there' before, not even her own husband.

The examination went very well, but just as he was finishing the doctor said: 'I would like to thank you for making such a big effort.'

Sally's friend and her mother discussed this afterwards. Could it just be because Sally's friend's mother was so clean? Eventually, they went through to the bathroom and looked through the cupboard to see the lotions the mother had used.

Imagine Sally's friend's horror when she realised her mother had sprayed her pubic hair with green glitter spray for the doctor. When she went into work the next day, everyone was laughing about her mother's private parts and how when her legs were wide open, they were lit up like a Christmas tree.

Sally and I laughed too, although I stopped after a while.

'Why did your friend have glitter in her bathroom anyway?' I asked, but Sally says I'm too literal.

Now I can't stop wondering if she sprays herself with glitter for Colin.

See *Indecent Exposure, Sex*

God

I used to spend a long time listening out for messages from God. Despite what the nuns said, I thought I had a vocation and if I didn't concentrate, I might miss the sign.

In the same way, I used to check my hands for stigmata every morning.

I never got a message. I know now this was a blessing. Imagine if you did spot the Star of Bethlehem one night on your way back from a club. Could you really tell anyone without being locked up? Or what if your sign was so stupid, it made people laugh? Like that Victorian couple who also gave up a lot of their lives to listening out for God. When the message finally came, they were beside themselves with excitement. They probably told all their friends, so imagine their humiliation when they eventually deciphered it.

'Eat more slowly,' God told them.

See *Ambition, Codes, Phantom E-mails*

Gossip

Every time Brian finds me talking to someone at work, he tells me off for being a gossip, but why is it that two men found talking together are discussing something important but two women are always gossiping?

See *Boxing, Glitter, Moustache, Women's Laughter*

Grief

There was a little boy in the park the other day. He was dressed in the full England kit, like a miniature footballer. He even had those long socks on and when he ran, he did that sideways swagger at the hips men do to make it look as if they aren't properly running. Just getting to somewhere quickly.

But then he fell over and his face went all square. Not just the shape of his face, but every little feature in it went square. His mouth was the most obvious. It turned into a letterbox in the middle of this red block. But even his eyes looked like small angular black stamps. His whole body went rigid too and when his shoulders shook, they turned into straight lines that went up and down, up and down, like a lift. I watched as his mother ran up and tried to get hold of him. It was difficult for her at first because his edges were too sharp, but then he suddenly deflated into a rag doll and she picked him up and took him over to the bench and made him happy again.

Just like that. I saw how she made him happy. One second he was crying and the next he was pointing at a dog and laughing.

I think the secret is in getting the tears out. Some mornings I wake up, and I know I've been crying in my sleep, but I just can't get the tears out. That's when you think you're drowning. You're not sharp or square. Just an empty outline filled up to the brim with lukewarm water that numbs everything inside you. You're too full to take anything in, and too blocked to let anything out. That's grief. Everything else is just sadness, and seeing a funny dog can make you better.

See *Happiness, Illness, Why?, You*

Gwyneth Paltrow

If I looked like Gwyneth Paltrow, nothing else could possibly go wrong in my life. And that's all I want to say about her. Basically.

See *Breasts, Star Quality*

H

Hair

My hair is very long and black. There's a little nub of black at the end of each strand. Like a small pool of ink. I can squash it between two pieces of paper so it sticks and leaves a dark streak when you press on it. I can even write with it. Sometimes I find marks I have left in books and forgotten about. Once I even did it to a library book. If I am ever captured, I will be able to write a note with my hair. It is the one advantage brunettes have over blondes.

Actually, I have started to pull my hair out. Each time I tug at a strand, there is a second when I don't think I'm going to be able to bear the pain. It's the only thing I can think about, but it never lasts long enough. When it's over, I flick the hair to the ground and immediately pull at another.

I was trying on some clothes the other day and I saw what I thought was a bald patch at the back of my head in the mirror. My legs nearly buckled, but when I went closer I saw that it was just the reflection from the light shining on my hair. I told myself that I would stop. Not that day, but one day soon.

When I was at school, I played netball with a girl called Susan Armstrong. One day she was just standing on the court itching her head and daydreaming. When the ball suddenly came towards her she put her hands up in panic to catch it, but she was still holding on to her hair and she yanked out a whole handful. It never grew back. The skin underneath was tighter and shinier than her face. It was like looking at the moon.

She couldn't have minded because she used to show it to everyone. Mind you, she was a bit of an exhibitionist. When she left school, she went to work in a fish and chip shop and had to wear a little hat over her head. Maybe it was because she couldn't let us see her bald patch any more that she would let us smell her arm. It was as if the oil and vinegar from all those fish suppers had soaked into her skin. I used to love smelling Susan's arm, but one day when there was no one else around I couldn't stop myself from leaning forward and licking her. Not hard. My tongue didn't actually reach the flesh, it just brushed the hairs on her arm backwards and forwards. I could almost feel each grain of salt in my mouth.

Susan kept her arm still and when I looked up into her face, I could swear I saw right through her eyes and into her soul. It was moon-like too, with patches waiting to be filled.

Even though she gave me extra chips that day, I never went back. I told everyone that I'd decided fish and chips weren't healthy.

See *Fashion, Lesbians, Visible*

Happiness

There is a new campaign at work which has been designed to expand the horizons of the support staff. This means that instead of the weekly gossipy lunch, we now have speakers who come in to talk about our personal development.

I enjoy most of these.

One of the best has been a man who came in and told us how to be happy. He said something that has stuck with me. He asked us what we'd do if we went into a room which had two doors leading from it. One had the notice on it which said 'Lecture on how to get to heaven' and the other said 'Heaven'. Which one would you go through?

We all thought about this, and more than half of us said that we'd go into the lecture first because it would make us better prepared. He laughed.

'Why not just go straight in?' he asked, and we couldn't tell him because then we would have had to admit that it was because we didn't feel quite up to heaven just at that moment. He was so confident. It was as if he'd been covered in shiny plastic that kept out all worries. Even his teeth looked as if they'd been carved from white rubber. You felt if you were to punch him, your fist would bounce right back and smack you one in the face. And you'd probably deserve it.

He told us that we had to write our obituaries. I tried all afternoon, but Brian kept leaning across and reading it out to everyone. Monica must have told him about the sex party, because he keeps calling me Glenda and winking. I think Brian is the kind of person who would read other people's diaries.

See *Grief, Kindness, Impostor Syndrome, Positive Thinking, Wobbling*

Heroines

One of my heroines is Grace Darling, the lighthouse keeper's daughter. This is not only because she had trouble with her hair. In fact, she and I have much else in common, including growing up with unsupportive mothers.

I first developed a craze on Grace when we went on holiday to Bamburgh. Every time I walked along by the sea, I would see the lighthouse at Longstone where she lived. I used to call her secretly 'my Grace' although she would never have played with me, of course.

No, I'll never forget visiting the Grace Darling museum and hearing her story for the first time. It wasn't that she risked her life to save all those people that startled me, it was the similarities between us. For a long time, I wondered if she had been reincarnated into me and took to wearing a shawl over my clothes until my mother stole it one night and refused to give it back because she said I was making a fool of myself.

It was Grace who saw me through this crisis. I thought of how her mother had tried to force her to finish her breakfast when she wanted to go out to sea straight away. And then to cap it all, her mother's last words to Grace were, 'Oh Grace, if your father is lost, I'll blame a' you for this morning's work.'

This didn't stop her sharing in the glory when it came. She even got a jug sent to her by a well-wisher with the inscription 'For the Mother of Grace Darling'. I would love it if my mother had received something like that. 'For Verity Bell's Mother'.

In fact, my mother is just one of the reasons that I have never been able to carry out any heroic actions. That, plus no one ever needed saving during all the time we stayed at Bamburgh.

But yes, I have always liked and empathised with strong women.

See *Boxing, Marathons, Voices, Weight*

Horoscopes

The other day I noticed a worrying thing. I have got into the habit of looking up Sally's horoscope before mine. It's a good job I don't believe in them anyway because I am a Taurus and we never seem to have much fun. Besides, Saturn is fighting Mars this week, and I need to watch my back at work. Someone will be hiding a deep secret from me. I didn't read Sally's properly but I did notice that not everyone close to her will have her best interests at heart. She refuses to tell me what star sign Colin is born under, but I bet it's Sagittarius. I have never trusted Sagittarians. They are too popular.

See *Omens, Questions*

Horror Movies

The only horror movie I have ever enjoyed was one that I went to with Sally. When we first started earning money, we'd go into London to spend the day shopping and sometimes fit in an early film. One day, I wanted to go and see a re-run of *The Sound of Music* in Leicester Square but somehow Sally got the wrong tickets and we ended up in the cinema next door.

Sally wouldn't let me leave straight away although she promised I could if I really, really hated the film but I'd have to go home on my own. She also said she'd hold my hand if I got scared. The heroine was a beautiful female photographer who saw death through her camera lens. Eventually the murderer she watched came after her in real life.

Something funny happened in the cinema that night. It was as if every one of us in the audience had been plugged into each other. The film can't have been that scary, but we all screamed as one, clung to complete strangers and at the end, when the murderer was climbing up the stairs to kill the photographer, we all started shouting at her to 'turn around and get the gun' at the top of our voices. It was exhilarating. When the film finally ended, all of us were laughing in our seats, none of us seemed to have the energy to move, and the cinema bars were full of people who wanted to talk about what had just happened.

Sally and I giggled for the whole of the train journey home, and when I woke up the next morning I knew that something wonderful had happened. I'd been part of something. I felt a deep sense of anti-climax for a long time afterwards.

See *Danger, God, Sculpture, Why?*

Houses

Most Saturdays, our family would go and look at the houses in the area which were up for sale.

It was a hobby, because we could never really afford any of the ones we looked at. When we saw one we particularly liked we would spend the week afterwards talking together about which piece of furniture would go where. We'd have arguments trying to decide what colour we would paint each room, which would be my bedroom, where my mother would sit and read in the evenings.

Sometimes I'd watch my parents walk round someone else's house hand-in-hand and I'd know what it was like to feel secure.

One house we saw was perfect. It started singing to us the minute we walked in. My mother and father opened cupboards in the large kitchen, sat on the window seat and watched where the sun fell, stood in silence looking at the view from the bedroom. I went downstairs to leave them in peace and found a room we hadn't gone into before.

It was extraordinary. Inside, every wall was covered in doors, all hung in identical white-painted doorframes. I opened one at random and all that was behind it was the wallpaper. I opened another, and then another, but all I could find was nothingness. It took me a long time to find the right door, the door out, and by the time I did I was crying.

No one spoke in the car on the way home, and when I followed my father inside I watched him kick our kitchen table when he thought no one was looking. My parents were upset that they couldn't afford the house, but I was pleased. It took me a long time before I could open a door without a feeling of dread, but when I told my father about it, he wouldn't believe me.

See *Doors, Kitchen Equipment, Magazines, Property, True Romance, Yellow*

I

Ice Cream

When I was six, I was taken to see *The Railway Children* but had to leave half-way through because I put my ice cream down the neck of the woman sitting in front of me. The funny thing is that I still want to do the same every time I go to the cinema. Just to see what will happen.

I used to like to bite off the end of my cone and suck the ice cream out that way. It upsets me nowadays to see that even advertisements for ice creams are using sex to make them appealing.

I once gave up sex for a whole year. It was amazing how much extra time I had. It wasn't that I was doing it all the time. It was the side-effects. If you're not interested in sex, then there's hardly a book, a film, a piece of music that you need to bother with. There are so many more hours in the day.

See *Glitter, Sex, Victim, Zero*

Illness

I hate being ill.

Other people at work have what they call 'duvet days', but I think they're probably the ones who have never come across really sick people. Otherwise they wouldn't pretend.

When my mother was in hospital, my father and I used to go and visit her every day. We would take a picnic for after our visit and have it in the little garden by the side of the car park. It became important that every day we'd have the same things to eat. Cheese and ham sandwiches, apples, and to wash it down, we'd share a bottle of sparkling water.

My father would just sit there and cry silently. The tears would roll down his cheeks and he'd not do anything to stop them. Sometimes people would look at us and then stare sympathetically at me, which confused me because Dad's tears were something you stopped noticing after a while.

I used to talk to Dad, not about emotions or anything. I stuck to facts. I'd tell him how many trees were in the garden. How much every separate item of our lunch had cost. I'd read out the football scores to him, right through to the third division. I'd go through the television guide, what was on each channel – even the digital ones which we didn't have. He'd nod away to me so he'd seem to be listening but then he'd turn and say something like: 'Your mum was so beautiful. I never knew what she saw in me. Even now, every time she goes out of the door, I think she won't bother to come back. She always seemed so precious. I was scared to touch her, you know. Scared I'd break her or something.'

Then we'd go back up to the ward and I'd look at Mum and try to see what he'd seen in her. We were never sure how much she took in but the nurses said it was important to keep trying to stimulate her. I'd tell her some of the things I'd just told Dad and he'd nod away again, as if I was right. As if he remembered. And then he'd touch her hand and I saw that he still saw her as precious. Was still worried he might lose her. She became whiter and whiter the longer she stayed in hospital, until she seemed to become part of the hospital bed. Her skin was as papery-dry and transparent as the sheet. Dad and I got browner though from all the picnic lunches we had in the sun until one day I looked at their hands together and it seemed Mum had already died. Her hand looked like a marble effigy next to his.

When Dad went into hospital not long afterwards, it seemed like a cruel joke. Some of the nurses even remembered us. I sat in the garden on my own then although Sally came with me a few times. She took me out for lunch once. We had chips, I remember, and my tears kept flowing. Just like Dad's.

Eventually the waiter came over. 'Is everything all right?' he asked. I guess he was worried I'd cause a scene or something.

Sally was wonderful. She looked him up and down and then she said: 'No. Everything is not all right. These chips have upset my friend very much. Can't you see how sad they have made her?'

We laughed then. It was the first time I'd laughed for

about a year and I had been afraid I'd forgotten how to, but when we got back to the hospital they told us Dad had passed away while we were out. He'd just given up the fight, they said. But I knew he'd died of a broken heart.

This is why I would never pretend to be ill to have a day off work.

See *True Romance*

Impostor Syndrome

There was another interesting speaker at work. She told us that we had to believe we were worthy of our positions in life, but that just made us laugh because she didn't seem to understand that most of us secretaries think the opposite – that we're actually much better than the position we've ended up in.

Still, she also said a lot of things that made sense. She said that many women have this arrow hanging over them. They think at any minute someone is going to walk in to where they're standing – whatever it is they're doing, even if (especially if) they're in the middle of something important – and tell them that they've been found out. That they're not good enough to continue. Please could they leave the room and let someone better carry on in their place.

My body felt electric. I couldn't believe other people have this arrow too. It follows you around, pointing at you in a crowd, and tells you exactly what you are doing wrong. Sooner or later someone is going to spot it too and realise exactly how useless you are. Probably when you have a mouthful of cheese sandwich and can't defend yourself.

It was reassuring to know this is just a syndrome. I could tell the others felt so too. They were more cheerful that afternoon than when they were writing their obituaries although I have noticed this personal development has encouraged us to talk about our feelings more. I am not sure this is altogether a good thing. What happens when it all goes wrong and there's nowhere to hide?

See *Codes, Happiness, Teaching, Why?*

Indecent Exposure

It is a fact of life about moving to a town, even one as small as this, that men are always exposing themselves to you. I feel rather like a nurse must feel about this. You see this little thing curled up like a shrimp and the expectant male face above it, waiting for you to react, and most of the time, it's not remotely sexy or even frightening. Just a bit boring.

Sally has a number of set phrases designed to wither a man at fifty paces, but that seems rather unnecessary. We're all just trying our hardest to survive – admittedly some more than others.

See *Boxing, Weight*

Influences

My mother was a great one for lists. She even spoke in bullet points.

'And another thing,' she'd say. Even when she was in full flow of one of her furies, she could tick off on her fingers all the points that made her angry.

The list she particularly loved was all the bad influences on me. I was easily led, that was my problem.

1.   Every English teacher I'd ever had. Especially Mr Shepherd in Year Ten, who wanted to take me and Marian Riley on a camping holiday in his two-man tent after we'd been reading Thomas Hardy in class. We were going to go to Dorset and explore Hardy country, but my mother wouldn't let me go.

2.   Suzanne Gibson. I never really understood this one. Suzanne lived in a hotel because her house had been repossessed when her father couldn't pay the bills any more. I always lived in fear that my mother would accuse Suzanne publicly of being a bad influence on me because Suzanne might think I'd been telling people we were friends when in fact she had never even bothered to look at me. She was far too glamorous.

3.   The Cathy and Claire column in *Jackie* magazine. Mum had read it once and been shocked by the sex advice offered. She never knew I'd written to them, explaining how I'd fallen in love with a girl in the Lower Sixth. I got a letter back from them saying it was just a crush and I

should join more sporting clubs to broaden my interests and make me a more rounded person.

4. Mr and Mrs Goodman, Sally's parents. They were always too jolly and family-oriented for my mother. Apparently it was a sign of how common they were. I hadn't realised until then that only common people are happy. It is posher as well as more interesting to be haunted by internal ghosts who make you miserable. Strangely, my mother liked Sally. She thought she'd come to a bad end and was therefore a good example for me of what not to do.

See *Danger, Telephone Boxes, Underwear, Zzzz*

J

Jacuzzi

I have always liked the idea of meeting someone in a jacuzzi. Of falling in love surrounded by shiny bubbles. Plus, when you've just swum yourself into a trance, you leave the rest of the world behind you. Relaxing after this is when I think you'd be able to talk about anything.

In our local swimming pool, they turn the top lights off after nine o'clock at night, and start playing country music through the loudspeakers. All the kids have gone home and there's only adults left, ploughing up and down the lengths, listening to words of love and lit up from below the water so they look like gods.

See *Impostor Syndrome, Mistaken Identity*

Jealousy

Why does Sally have to be given so much in life?

It doesn't really help her. She takes so much for granted.

She complains about things as if she really doesn't care about them. She says she wants to live on her own and doesn't want to be beholden to anyone. She wants no possessions, no ties, no responsibilities. She says this is her ambition. But you can only really leave things behind if you have them in the first place – a family, a relationship, opinions. Otherwise you're not even running away. You're merely existing somewhere, anywhere, else.

Still, the good thing is that I am not at all jealous of Sally. We each bring our own attributes to the relationship which are mutually beneficial. I am completely happy with my own life. I wish Sally well in hers.

Sally and I are friends. No, no, no. I am not jealous of Sally. I am especially not jealous of Sally's relationship with Colin.

See *Zzzz*

John

I can't wait to tell Sally.

The most amazing thing has happened.

I have fallen in love. I feel glowing. I feel fantastic. I have just walked down the street and everybody smiled at me. Men whistled at me. I feel like a goddess. I look down at my arms and my skin looks as if it has been sprinkled with diamond dust.

Everybody is so much nicer, funnier, prettier. And so am I.

His name is John.

K

Kate

John has a wife. Sally told me first. Well, she didn't know exactly but what she said was if he e-mails you from work, he is married. If it is always him who has to call you, he has children. If he doesn't have any hobbies, it is because he has a family life, not no life.

I asked John but he was going to tell me anyway. Straight after we talked about it, he asked me to tell him a joke, so I believe him when he says being married isn't a problem.

'Two parrots were on a perch,' I said. 'One said to the other, "Can you smell fish?"'

Sally told me this joke. It made everyone else laugh but I can't really understand it. I think it might be surrealist. When I asked John this, he told me I was funny and he loved me. He couldn't tell me why that should surprise him so.

John's wife's name is Kate. I don't like the way they're

next to each other in the alphabet. My name is Verity so I'm right at the end, out of the way.

He doesn't love her. He never has. They are together just for the sake of the children.

See *Women's Laughter*

Kindness

I want to go round the world carrying out random acts of kindness. I want to buy extravagant foods and leave them on pensioners' doorsteps. I want to get up on a snowy day and wipe the windscreens of every car in the street. I want to entertain small children so their mothers can sleep. I want to take every homeless person to the Ritz for a night. I want to hire the Bolshoi Ballet and put on performances in Trafalgar Square so commuters can be inspired on their way to work. I want to stand on street corners and wait for blind men to come along so I can lead them across the street. I want to tape the wings of injured birds with lolly sticks and Band-Aids. I want to distribute food to orphans, take guns off soldiers, rid the world of nuclear threats.

I want everyone to feel as happy as I do. I am so fucking happy I think I'm going to explode.

See *Grief, Impostor Syndrome, Nostrils*

Kisses

I've taught John to do that twiddly thing with his tongue that the Australian did. He should be in one of those kissing booths at village fêtes. I am sure there are many, many people who would pay to be kissed like that.

The funny thing is I sold my first kisses for money. My mother would slip me cash for kissing my grandmother whenever we went to visit her. I would have done it for free, but I pretended I didn't like touching her prickly, hairy old-lady cheeks because it seemed to give my mother pleasure. In fact, I wanted to rub my skin against my grandmother's for ever. She smelt of lavender and dried rosebuds and those thin tubes of Parma Violet sweets. Very different from my mother, who had a tinny chemical smell that stung you when you got too close.

When my grandmother was small, she won a book for good attendance at her Sunday School. She kept it very carefully on a small pine shelf with the few books she had, and I was never allowed to look at any of them. For some reason, this shelf was in her bathroom.

One day when I was staying with her, I crept up to the bathroom and read it. It was called *Freddy's Little Sister* and was all about a boy who was forced to beg on the streets because his parents had died. He needed food to look after his little sister who was all he had in the world, but no one gave him any money and everyone was horrible. Just when you thought it couldn't get any worse, Freddy's Little Sister died. Then the book ended. I cried and cried and cried, and wouldn't talk to my grandmother all evening. Eventually she hit me because she realised I had read her special book.

If I had a brother like Freddy, she wouldn't have done that. I told John about it and he held me so close.

See *Baked Beans, Breasts, Endings, Zest*

Kitchen Equipment

John and I met through work. This is just one of the reasons we have to keep things quiet. In one of our newsletters, we ran a competition to find the top chambermaid for our client, who supplied cleaning materials to hotel chains. Third prize was a full range of non-stick saucepans. Because it wasn't very important, Brian let me organise the photograph of the girl receiving her prize from John who was the representative of the kitchen equipment company. It was a bit embarrassing because Maureen wasn't as pleased with her prize as I thought she should be. She even complained about how she was going to get all the pans back home on the train with her to Leicester, which I have to admit was something we hadn't thought of. Eventually I got her a taxi to the station, and when we found she'd left the 9-inch frying pan behind, John said I could keep it, which was nicer than he should have been given the circumstances. I think it was his kindness I fell in love with first.

When John rang me up at work the next week, he sounded nervous, as if I wouldn't remember who he was. But I did. We arranged to go out for a drink that evening and he said that if I didn't remember what he looked like, I wasn't to worry because he always went everywhere with a full set of saucepans and this was a fairly good distinguishing mark. I was a bit puzzled until I realised this was his sense of humour. What John didn't know was that I'd asked the photographer to print out an extra copy of the pan presentation photograph and pinned it above my desk. Brian still thinks it's because it's the first job I've done by myself. He tells me he finds my enthusiasm refreshing.

See *John, Liqueur Chocolates, Objects, Vacuuming*

L

Lesbians

Poor John. He has to put up with so much. He told me in strict secrecy that he thinks his wife might be a lesbian.

Apparently, she and her women friends touch a lot, even in front of him. They call each other things like doll and poppet and petal, and are always sending secret e-mails. When John comes in, Kate hides what she's writing so he knows it is probably about him. He has to pretend not to mind otherwise she'll tease him.

He says the worst thing is how these women are always laughing when they are together. John says he hardly laughs any more. It's all work and duty as far as he's concerned. That's why he loves being with me. He can feel appreciated.

He says Kate and her friends only seem to care about having fun. He honestly thinks that if it came down to it, she would choose her friends over him.

'It's not like you and Sally,' he says. 'You're like blokes. You can pick up and drop your friendship when there's nothing better to do.'

I talk about this with Sally. She says that Colin lives in hope of walking in and finding Sally and me in a delicate situation together. It is his deepest fantasy. I'm so grateful John understands friendship for what it is, and is not always trying to turn it to his advantage. This is so typical of Colin, and also of Sally not to mind.

See *Codes, Rude, Voyeur, Women's Laughter*

Letters

Dear Kate
I think you should know that . . .

Dear Mrs Hutchinson
Your husband and I have been . . .

To Whom It May Concern
John Hutchinson is in love with . . .

Dear Kate
I hope you will forgive me for remaining anonymous but I am a well-wisher who . . .

Dear Kate Hutchinson
I have thought long and hard before writing this letter but . . .

Dear Wife of John
I . . .

Dear.
Oh dear.

See *Codes, Endings, Utopia*

Liqueur Chocolates

John sometimes finds it difficult to use the L-word. We have used up the apricot liquid I won at the sex party, but the other day he broke open liqueur chocolates on my bare skin and made a joke of it. 'I lllll you' he said, sticking out his tongue and licking the spilt liqueur off instead of saying love. It was fun at the time but I was disappointed afterwards. And sticky. Sally says the thing to do is not to nag. They get enough of that at home.

'What has he brought you?' she asked. 'These men just love buying us presents, don't they?'

I couldn't show her the frying pan, the set of matching cookie tins or even the tea towel with illustrations of all the different species of fish. Even though John and I chose it together from the fish and chip shop we call our local, it doesn't match Colin's presents. Not in cash terms any-how. I use the tea towel to wrap up the empty chocolate boxes. John says we've got a habit.

See *Glenda G-Spot, Tornados*

Love Calculators

There is a webpage on the internet that lets you type in your name and the name of the person you love and it works out whether you are a good match or not. John and I are 67 per cent compatible. Dr Love says that we need to work at our relationship. Sally and Colin have distinct possibilities at 78 per cent, but on the other hand, Colin and I are 99 per cent right for each other. A match made in heaven.

When I was at school, we didn't go on computers so much, so we used pen and paper instead. We'd cross out all the letters that appeared in both names and then work our way through the remainder chanting out love/hate. When I try this with John's name, I realise that we only have two letters in common although the ones we do share spell IT, which has to be significant. However, when I do the rhyme, it comes out hate. I don't know John's middle name though. Maybe if I used our full names, it would come out with a more correct answer.

See *Mistaken Identity*

Lust

When my father was lying in his hospital bed, I tried hard to concentrate on things he'd like to talk about. It was difficult though because what I couldn't say was how I felt I was wading through an erotic fever. The sicker he got, the more I wanted to make love to healthy men. My need was shaming. John was the first person I told about how I really felt. The men I knew at the time were too grateful to speak much anyway. When John told me lots of people felt the same, I was so relieved. This is what I like about John, not the fact that being with him is exciting, just the opposite. John makes me feel normal.

See *Grief, Illness, Teaching, Why?*

M

Magazines

John thinks it is strange that I have never shared a flat with anyone. I did think about moving in with Sally once but then Mum got ill, so I just stayed at home until I bought my own flat.

Besides, having a flatmate is not something I've ever fancied. It's not just all that fridge etiquette, but if I wanted to sum up everything I hate about the flatmate relationship, it's the way they read each other's brand-new magazines without asking. There is something so special about opening a glossy magazine and being the first to tear the pages when they get stuck together, or try out the perfumes. A used magazine is about as appealing as a half-finished yoghurt. At least I know Sally would never leave me with either.

See *Houses, Routines, Velvet*

Marathons

The first time John and I had sex over the telephone, it was just a joke. Now, we do it for hours. He once rang me up from the supermarket car park when he was supposed to be picking up some barbecue meat. He'd gone into the far corner where no one could see him. It felt incredibly sexy and strong for me to turn him on so much. I felt liberated.

I told him we'll have to get each other those special hands-free microphones for Christmas. He said we will get so used to talking about sex that when we finally get together we will have to have separate phonelines installed in the house so we can carry on doing it this way.

When we finally get together.

I didn't say anything at the time, but I was desperate for him to get off the line so I could phone Sally. When I did, I could tell from her tone that Colin had never said anything like that to her.

See *Boxing, Endings, Heroines, Jealousy, Ultimatum, Why?, Youth*

Mars Bars

Sally and I used to buy Mars bars from the school tuckshop. Then we would wrap them in wet flannels and put them on the radiator so they'd get a mottled, almost mouldy, look. We became experts at writing disappointed complaint letters to the company using different names, and we'd get sent large selection boxes in recompense. It was fine at first, but the trouble was that we got greedy and the company got the school tuck-shop shut down because they had received so many complaints about its hygiene.

We never told anyone it was us. Especially when everyone got so annoyed about not being able to buy snacks any more. They might have forgiven Sally, but never me.

See *Blackbirds, Robins and Nightingales, Outcast, Vendetta*

Memory

– Will you love me for ever?
– I will.
– Will you ever forget me?
– Never.
– Will you remember me in one week's time?
– Of course.
– Will you remember me in one year's time?
– Definitely.
– Will you remember me in ten years' time?
– I will.
– Knock, knock.
– Who's there?
– See, you've forgotten me already.
– Jesus, woman, just let me read the paper, can't you? This is worse than being with the kids.
–
– Verity?
–

– Verity, oh Verity, darling. Stop crying. I didn't mean it. I'll remember you for ever. I promise. I'll love you for ever.

See *Endings*

Mirrors

A funny thing happened when I looked in the mirror this morning.

I saw I had tilted my head slightly to the left without thinking, and for a minute it was my mother looking back at me. I was even making that half smile she made every time she looked in the mirror, as if she was greeting someone she hadn't seen for a long time.

This might be a sign of age. I have noticed that the older women at work always put their heads to one side when they look in the mirror. It's as if they're afraid of what they'll see if they face themselves straight on.

See *Daisies, Horror Movies, Mistaken Identity, Old, Voyeur, Zzzz*

Mistaken Identity

I once pretended to be my mother on the telephone. I didn't mean to do it. It was just that the person on the other end automatically assumed I was Mrs Bell. It felt wonderful, just like when I used to take my father's car keys and walk up and down swinging them in my hand, hoping that people would think I was old enough to own a car. I started to feel that if only I really could take my mother's place, everything would be all right. I would have somewhere to go where I could be me.

Maybe this is what we always feel about mothers. Their very presence stops us being us. Maybe this is why I hate Kate so much.

From what John says she has always put being a mother first. She has been too busy with the kids to spend any time with him for a long time. She has no idea of how much he needed her, and now they have nothing in common but the children. I can't help thinking this is the wrong thing for her to do when mothers are so easily replaced.

See *Daisies, Engagement Ring, Illness, The Queen II, Stepmothers, Underwear*

Money

Not many people know that if you put a two-pound coin in the freezer and wait until it is completely frozen, you can then press the middle bit out with your thumbs.

Mind you, this makes it difficult to use, so you can only do this if you have money to spare.

John has started talking about money a lot. It makes me feel uncomfortable because we have such different ideas about it. He thinks if he ever had any spare cash, it would be his duty to spend as much of it as he could. Not just on himself, but on making other people happy. I told him that when I was young, I always used to be very helpful to old people on buses because I thought they might then leave all their money to the little girl who was so kind to them. Every time I heard the doorbell ring, I would wonder whether this was my reward coming. Now John says that he wants money so he can leave it to a complete stranger when he dies. Maybe someone whose name he pulls out of a phone book at random and who will always be perplexed by why he or she was chosen.

See *Love Calculators, Surnames, Utopia*

Money – Even More of It

Of course, when my parents died and left me an inheritance, I knew why they chose me. I just didn't expect it to be so much. Money wasn't something we ever talked about at home. Even the solicitor was surprised. He kept going on about the Responsibility. About how I was an 'heiress' now. It made me think of Joan Crawford somehow. All hard and glittery but with enough shoulder pads to bear all that Responsibility.

Everyone was so kind to me after my father passed away. Sally took me home and I slept in their spare room for a week. Her mother made me cups of tea and her father teased me, and every time I cried they thought it was because I was sad about my parents. They didn't realise it was because I was so comfortable there. This is what I wanted for the rest of my life. And I couldn't bear the guilt of that.

This is why I don't want the money. It changes everything. Sally's parents would expect me to check into a hotel, not take me under their wing like they did. I worked it out with my solicitor that no one need know anything about it. We've let out the house through a letting agency, and what with that, and the income from my stocks and shares, I don't need to worry about anything any more. He even gives me pocket money as if he's my father. He insists I go to his office every month to go through things although I trust him absolutely and only pretend to check the figures.

The trouble is you can't go to bed with money. It can't hug you and stroke you and tell you that everything is going to be all right. As soon as you have it, it covers you up so everyone expects you to take charge. To be the one to tell everyone else that everything is going to be all right. To take the Responsibility.

In fact, my solicitor is the only person who knows about the legacy. Sometimes, if I try very hard, I can forget about it myself. I can even enjoy dreaming with John how we would spend our imaginary millions. This has become one of our favourite topics of conversation. Sometimes I wonder if it is what holds us together. We have such plans that would all come true if only we had the money.

See *Danger, Jealousy, Teaching, Velvet, Yields*

Moustache

I had the idea to make a giant heart out of chicken wire and fill it with white fairy lights as a surprise for John. I went to the hardware shop to get the stuff but wasn't sure what wire cutters to buy. When I asked someone, I suddenly found myself surrounded by four men offering me different advice. They were all very interested in what I was doing, and two of them even offered to come round and help me if I hit problems.

On my way home, it struck me that I had stumbled upon something important. Women spend all this time and money on finding Mr Right. What they don't realise is that men are there all the time, lurking in the aisles of DIY shops. All you have to do is buy wire cutters.

I think I am finally coming to understand the secrets between men and women. John was feeling around my face with his fingertips the other night. He traced the outline of my nose, pressing the end with his thumb. He told me that his mother used to do this when he was a little boy so he would have a round nose like hers, and not his father's beak.

He then rested all his fingertips over my upper lip. 'I love your moustache,' he said. I felt myself go tense, especially when he leant forward and dolloped out little butterfly kisses all over my face. Was he joking?

I pushed him away. 'What's wrong?' he asked. He really couldn't understand.

'I haven't got a moustache,' I said. 'Men have moustaches, not women.'

'But you've got such a wonderful one,' John said. 'It's beautiful. You've no idea how it turns me on. I wish you wouldn't pluck out the hairs like you always do.'

I couldn't believe it. I have spent so many years trying to hide the fact that I have facial hair, and here was someone telling me it was sexy. My stomach turned over with love for John. If only men realised that this was all women needed. To be desired without boundaries, to be loved for all the things we have got wrong with us, not for what we would like to be.

See *Hair, Vacuuming, Women's Laughter*

Mystery Tours

My father was brought up in a cathedral city and when he used to take Mum off for their little holidays, I would stay with my grandparents there. In the cathedral, there was an effigy of a dead body that had been carved after the body was buried and dug up. It had worms coming out from its skull. My grandmother would always take me to see it, and then leave me there while she went shopping.

As another special treat we would go to the department store where there was a cage of stuffed birds. If you put a penny in, they would come to life and sing to you. I got told off once for hitting a small boy who just stood by, watching the birds sing, while I used up all my pocket money. Maybe, my grandmother said afterwards, he didn't have any money and that was his only chance of happiness. Don't you feel guilty because you have so much?

I thought about this a lot and even though I didn't have any pudding that day, I was still glad I hit him.

Once she took me on a mystery tour. We had to get on a coach in the town centre first thing in the morning, and we didn't have a clue where we were going. The coach was full of old people and my grandmother kept telling me how exciting it was. We went down so many bumpy roads I started to feel sick, but we drove and drove and drove until we came to a pub and the coach driver got out and had a drink. My grandmother bought me a warm lemonade and some crisps and then when I went to the loo, a wasp drowned in my lemonade. I couldn't have another because it was time to drive back home. When I called my parents that evening, my grandmother shouted to me that I should tell them what fun we had. So I did.

For years afterwards, everyone kept telling me how much I enjoyed mystery tours until I nearly believed them.

See *Dreams, Jealousy, Kisses, Underwear*

N

Names

My father told me that when he was growing up there was a family in his road who called their sons by the days of the week and their daughters by the months of the year. They only reached June with the girls but the boys went right through the week. My father's particular friend was called Saturday Smith.

We used to talk about names a lot in our family. That's what makes me realise how much they matter. Once my father hit the dining-room table with the flat of his hand because he'd got into a blind rage about why someone would call their child James James. That's what got me thinking that maybe your name becomes more important than something you just have dangling down from your head, like a scarf, or a handbag. Your name gets into your lifeblood, so a Jane is always going to be different from a Mercedes. A Daisy from a Violet. A Kate from a Verity.

In which case, it worries me even more how many Conservative politicians are called Norman.

'How many people do you know called Norman?' I asked John one night. He said he knew no one personally.

'Now think how many Conservatives you can name,' I said. 'They even marry Normas. Is this something that happens at birth, or do you turn Conservative from years of being bullied at school?'

John tells me that he was at school with someone who wanted to be a spy. This boy would never let himself be photographed in case it could be used against him later. John can't remember his name, even when I tell him I was at school with a girl called Jackie Gotobed.

See *Codes, Surnames, Words*

New Men

Sally and I agree that we could never love a new man. It's not just the sandals either. It's the lack of juice. You want to feed them raw steak. John says that what he loves most about me is the way I desire him. He says it makes him feel real. I can't talk about this with Sally. She'd think I was just a sex object for John.

See *Marathons, Phone Calls, Rude, Sex*

Noddy

John was once sitting down watching television with his wife when he remembered a joke someone had told him.

He laughed so much his wife prodded him to shut up but John was so helpless with laughter, he rolled off the sofa and on to the carpet. He sobered up then, and got back up. Neither of them referred to the incident at all. They just carried on watching the programme. This has worried John for a long time, which is why I try to laugh with him at the joke, but if I'm honest I find it sad rather than funny. This is how it goes:

Noddy was going to see his good friend, Big Ears. He woke up in the morning and was very excited.

'Thank you, bed,' he said, 'for letting me sleep so well so I can be wide awake to see my good friend, Big Ears.'

And then he went to the bathroom.

'Thank you, bathroom,' he said, 'for letting me use you so I can be well prepared to see my good friend, Big Ears.'

And then he went to have some breakfast.

'Thank you, kitchen' he said, 'for being there so I can prepare food to give me energy to see my good friend, Big Ears. Thank you, food,' he said, as he ate, 'for filling me up so I can see my good friend, Big Ears. Thank you, floor,' he said as he crossed the room, 'for taking me to the door so I can see my good friend, Big Ears. Thank you, door,' he said as he went outside, 'for letting me out of the house to see my good friend, Big Ears.'

He went to his car. 'Thank you, car,' he said as he got in, 'for taking me to see my good friend, Big Ears.'

He drove along. 'Thank you, tarmac, thank you, pavement, thank you, traffic signals, thank you, map, thank you, road directions, thank you, thank you, thank you, everyone who is helping me see my good friend, Big Ears.'

He parked outside the house. 'Thank you, road, for letting me leave my car so I can see my good friend, Big Ears. Thank you, gate, for opening so I can go and see my good friend, Big Ears. Thank you, path, for taking me up to the house of my good friend, Big Ears. Thank you, doorbell, for letting me ring to alert my good friend, Big Ears.'

He waited until he could hear footsteps coming down the stairs inside the little house.

'Thank you, stairs,' he whispered, 'for bringing my good friend, Big Ears, closer and closer to me.'

At last, Big Ears opened the door.

'Fuck off, Noddy,' he said.

See *Doors, Houses, Liqueur Chocolates, Youth*

Normals

Last summer, Sally and I were on a train when we noticed that the two men in the seats across the aisle had not looked at us once.

This was puzzling.

I thought they must have been trainspotters, but Sally listened to their conversation for a bit. It turned out that what they actually spotted was the stations. They rode on trains every day choosing lines which took them through the highest number of stations. Then they wrote the names down in a big book.

We couldn't stop laughing. Every time we thought we'd got it under control, the train would glide past some deserted platform with one of those swinging signs and we'd hear the shuffle of papers opposite us and we'd be off again. We were crying and making little squeaks like baby pigs. Sally's nose was starting to run.

The men did look at us then. One of them even shrugged and spat out the word 'normals'.

I asked Brian about this the next day. He said that a friend of his who sometimes liked to go trainspotting, well anyway this 'friend' had heard that people who didn't like trainspotting were called Normals. I couldn't explain to Brian why I found this insulting. I just did.

He told me then that naturists – and another 'friend' of his apparently has been known to go to nudist beaches – called people who wore clothes Textiles. He kept on about this for the rest of the day as if it was a joke both of us shared.

'How are you doing, Textile?' he'd shout across from his desk.

The trouble with Brian is that he doesn't know when he has taken things too far.

See *Bosses, Firefighting, Glenda G-Spot, Words, Zero*

Nostrils

Sophia found me crying in the ladies at work. Of all the people to see me at my worst, she would be one of the last I'd pick. It's not just the fact that she is the company accountant. It's her nostrils. They're more on show than anyone else's. It's as if she's put two fingers up her nose and turned it inside out. They're long and stretched and the skin's boiled red inside. It's difficult to look at Sophia and think of anything else. I would hate to see Sophia with a cold. Just the thought of it makes me feel physically sick.

Sophia took me by the hand and led me into her office. She put me in a chair in the corner of the room and just ignored me. Eventually, I stopped sobbing and stood up.

'It won't be the last time it happens,' she said, barely looking at me. 'And every time it does, you will think this really is the end, that this time you'll never get back with each other, and your heart will break again and again until you don't think you can bear it any more. But I promise you that you've a long hard journey ahead. You won't be able to leave each other alone and it will hurt just as much each time one of you decides that you must part.'

'How did . . .'

'Oh, I don't know the details of your particular relationship,' she said. 'But I do know about pain indexes, believe me. And men. He won't be worth it. They never are.'

Then she handed me a mirror before going back to her columns of figures.

'You'd better freshen up,' she said. 'You look a mess.'

I stared at my reflection. My eyes were puffy and red, but who was she to call me a mess? At least I have always been lucky with the shape and size of my nostrils.

See *Friends, Kindness, Wrists*

Nursing

If I could change just one thing about John it would be the way he is always complaining about being ill. Last

Monday, for example, he was moaning about a pain in his arm.

'It is either a strain from all the gardening Kate made me do over the weekend, or the last stages of a cancerous tumour,' he whinged. I tried to take his mind off it, but I noticed he kept rubbing the spot and looking worried, as if he might die at any minute.

I told Sally about it. I shouldn't have done because she kept mocking John, rubbing her forehead and saying either she was bored with talking about him or she was in the last stages of a terminal tedium. But then she had a good idea.

Now whenever John complains about being ill, I am incredibly sympathetic. I tell him he should tell Kate to massage him gently for a long time, or to cook him special meals, or to go and buy him expensive and elusive medicines.

'Do you think so?' he asks, hopefully.

'I do,' I say. 'I think this is something she needs to take very seriously indeed. I would, if I were her.'

See *Illness, Stationery, Teaching, Women's Laughter*

O

Objects

John told me that he went round his house last night looking at all the objects he and his wife had bought together. He said he was ticking things off in his mind.

If I go, I'll take this, this and this.

That, that and that will stay.

It was a terrible thing to do, he said, because he realised that was all a marriage comes down to in the end. Objects. Even the children, he said. Even the children would be shared between him and Kate.

I held him close and told him that if I had him, I would never need anything else. We stayed like that, in each other's arms, for a long time. We were silent because he was upset, and all I wanted to ask was whether he was going to take the painting of beach huts by the sea that we once took to be reframed.

I have always liked that painting.

See *Houses, Money, Property, Questions*

Old

My heart is breaking. All I can see in front of me is a dark, black corridor with nothing to make it worthwhile coming out the other side. John can't bring himself to think about leaving Kate any more. He says it would kill her. Apparently she's spent too much of her life relying on him and he has to accept the responsibility. Plus he'd feel so guilty that he'd taken the best years of her life. Maybe if they'd both been younger? Younger like me. He told me that I'd be all right, that I had my whole life ahead. I had to live well, to make him proud.

I felt numb. He was crying when he said all this so I told him it was all right, that I understood, but the next day I was having a sandwich in a local coffee shop when I realised the woman sitting opposite me was in her early forties, probably exactly the same age as Kate. I knew it wasn't her, but I couldn't stop staring at this woman. She was reading some papers, an important-looking document, so I felt I could stare all I wanted without her noticing me.

I was trying to see what it was like to be that old. She had all the usual imperfections, but when I looked closely I saw some I hadn't thought of before. The skin at the side of her face was puckered round her ears as if it needed stretching. Then when she turned round to pick her coat off the back of the chair, I saw she had lines at the back of her neck as thick and deep as the gold chain she was wearing. The area round her eyes was black, not just underneath as you get sometimes from lack of sleep but at the edges of her nose right up to her eyebrows too, so her sockets looked sunken.

John told me once that what Kate hated most about getting old was the fact that she felt she was becoming invisible. John said that Kate was losing all her confidence and bounce. This was another thing that made him feel guilty.

I could see this woman was nervous. She apologised when other people bumped into her, she kept giving me silly little smiles, she tried to make conversation with the man who came to clear away the table even though he wasn't interested. When I saw her start to put her things away to go, I knocked over my coffee on purpose, willing the dark brown liquid to spill over her papers.

'I'm sorry,' I said, as she whipped everything up quickly, trying to get rid of the worst of the damage with a sodden paper napkin. 'I just didn't notice you there.'

The woman looked as if she was trying not to cry. The manager came rushing over. He was about twenty-five, as dark and handsome as an Italian film star. I smiled at him, and he stopped in his tracks for a moment, then smiled back. Together we watched the woman flutter her hands here and there until he remembered what he was there for and started to wipe the papers with the wet cloth in his hands.

'Don't.' She was almost shouting. 'These are important. They're Work things.' That's how she spoke. Gave Work a capital letter, as if that was all she had in her life. All she had left to her. After she'd gone, I watched the other people in the café give each other little smiles. I hoped she'd get into trouble when she got back to the office. I felt no guilt. Didn't she know it was women her age who were ruining my life?

The next night John came round and said he was wrong. That he couldn't let me go. That he'd see a way of making things all right. I made a point of lifting up my hair and asking him to kiss the back of my neck. I told him women loved that, because I guessed he sometimes tried out things we did with Kate. 'Is it smooth?' I asked. 'Are there any lines there?' He whispered into my skin that I was beautiful, flawless, a national treasure. I turned my head round so his mouth was against my cheek, just by my ear.

'I really couldn't bear to be lined and ugly,' I said. 'I'll be perfect for you for ever.'

He smiled, but something was wrong. It was the first time I'd been with John and felt guilty. He kept poking his tongue at my skin until I had to push him off.

See *Breasts, Endings, Mistaken Identity, Youth*

Omelette

My mother always used to say that it was impossible to make an omelette without breaking eggs. It seemed substantial at the time, like something I should listen to, but I can't help wondering what it all meant now. Of course you need to break the eggs. It's just common sense.

See *Elephant's Egg, Endings, Old, Questions, Voices, X*

Omens

The world has become a more interesting place since I fell in love.

A magpie flying over used to be just a black and white bird. It is now a sign that today is going to be awful so I have to spend the next hour searching for another to balance it out. Two birds flying together fill me with joy. It means that John really does love me. That we're going to be happy together for ever.

That black cat crossing the road . . . the chimney sweep . . . the four-leaved clover. If I go into a pub and count ten blond-haired men, if the sandwich I've picked with my eyes shut turns out to be chicken, if I can get to that shop without seeing a red car.

If.

See *Horoscopes, Love Calculators, Telephone Boxes, Utopia*

Only Children

Sally and I are both only children. John is the youngest of three. He has two children of his own. There are bound to be things he can't understand about me that Sally can.

There is a responsibility about being an only child. On the one hand, you are the most wanted person in the Universe, the completer of the family, the little plastic figure that makes living in the doll's house worthwhile. On the other, you bear single-handedly the pressure for changing someone's life beyond recognition. When things go wrong, it can be no one else's fault but yours.

This is a lot for a child to have to cope with.

There was a psychological experiment once. They put a group of strangers in a room and forbade them to speak to one another. Then they asked them to circle round, just looking, until they found someone they wanted as their potential partner. They all chose, but remember, they hadn't spoken yet. When they finally got to talk to their partner, the vast majority found that they had paired up with someone who shared the same place in the family as they did. Youngest child with youngest child, eldest with eldest, middles with middles. I like to think the experiment finally ended when the only children were peeled off the outside walls and forced to join in with the rest. Maybe they would then have made cynical comments about the easy comradeship of the other people there, but more likely they would have got into an argument as to who had the unhappiest childhood.

See *Ants, Blood, Captains, Daisies, Questions, Relatives, Zzzz*

Oranges

I knew a girl once who used to say that if you ever wanted to pick anyone up, all you needed to do was go on a train journey with a copy of *Rebecca* and a large apple. You would have hardly nibbled through the skin, or even reached Manderley, before a man approached you.

I tried it with John one evening but all I had in the fruit bowl was oranges. John was watching the football and he didn't even look at me, just passed me his hanky so I could mop the juices off my chin. He says it's a compliment to how relaxed he feels with me that he can spend the little time we have together watching television.

Besides, it was an important match that he was supposed to be watching down the pub with his friend, Sam.

See *Endings*

Orphans

I have been an orphan for two years now. It's difficult to say that without sounding pathetic, but my friends are now my family. Well, John is now my family.

No, I am completely happy. I miss nothing. I am searching for nothing. Especially not a father figure. Sally is wrong. She is just jealous because although Colin has more money, he does not treat her as well as John looks after me. I can tell John everything. And I do. He says he wants to protect me so carefully that no harm will ever happen to me. This is why I have to do what he says, be what he wants. Everyone needs someone to look after them.

See *Stepmothers, Teaching, Voices, Zzzz*

Outcast

Until we started on her, Dawn was no different from any other girl at school.

But then one day in the lunch hall, she dropped her tray. It was full of food, but while embarrassing, even that might have been all right on its own. After all, it was something we worried about doing ourselves, but then instead of cursing, or picking it up, or doing anything, Dawn just stood there, blushing. Soon she was completely red.

Dollops of shepherd's pie in greasy gravy lay around her feet. Chunks of tinned pineapple, banana, peach left snail trails on the floor where they'd skittered away from the shattered bowl.

After the initial thud, the dining hall was completely silent. Everyone was watching Dawn. I felt my stomach well up and get stuck in my throat. Why didn't she do anything? My head seemed to be expanding beyond my skull. I wanted to scream.

I don't know who it was who first started to clap, but soon we were all joining in. That slow clap-clap-clap, each one separated by a heartbeat's silence. Even the teachers seemed frozen, until Dawn span round and ran out of the hall. She must have kept on running through the school and into the street because the next time we saw her, she was standing next to her father as our form teacher told us all about how we must be kind to everyone, regardless of their background. How we mustn't ostracise Dawn just because she was not like us.

We stared at Dawn, trying to work out what was wrong with her background. I honestly don't think anyone had noticed anything special about her before. It was then that we saw the hole in her cardigan elbow, the dirty socks, the smudges on her face not wiped off by a mother's spit. She was looking down at the ground as if to give us a better view of the scruffy parting, not painfully sculpted each morning like our mothers did with the sharp end of the comb.

Then we started on her father. We asked ourselves what he was doing there in school when all our fathers were at work. Why was he in dirty old jeans and a V-necked jumper without a shirt, let alone a tie? We saw him looking at us all not defiantly but with eyes full of what we could recognise even then as defeat.

I can't remember anyone ever talking about it, but I can't have been the only one who felt my blood rise at how they could just stand there and take the humiliation. We became pack animals, the rest of us, trying to rid ourselves of the weakest links.

Dawn never had a happy day at school again after that. Sometimes she tried to talk to me because I was left on my own at playtime too, but I'd turn my back on her.

Couldn't she see that being hated was something two people could never have in common?

See *Captains, Startrite Sandals, Vendetta*

P

Pain Index

If John and I were together the whole time I know we would be able to speak normally to each other. The trouble is, when we speak on the telephone now, I have a second conversation – the things I really want to know – going on in my mind. This makes it difficult to talk, so when I do eventually say what I want to say it comes out too quickly and harshly and I start crying.

John says he can't bear it. He just wants things back to being as they were. He says I need to find a way round this.

See *Nostrils, Utopia*

Phantom E-mails

The first time I e-mailed myself, it was just a joke. To see what would happen.

Dear Verity, I wrote,
You are my life. Every time I wake up, I wish
you were next to me. Nothing is worth us being apart.

And then one click of a button and it was gone. I forgot
all about it, but the next time I checked my e-mails, I felt a
rush of joy when I saw there was one waiting for me in
my in-box.

It was everything I could have wanted. Brian must have
seen the smile on my face because he started teasing me. I
had to admit that yes, I had just received a wonderful
note. 'You are my life,' I whispered to myself. For the rest
of that day, everyone was nicer to me than they usually
were. I think they wanted to rub a little of my joy off on
to their own lives.

I kept checking all day but there wasn't another e-mail.
Late at night, after a bottle of wine, I went on to the internet
again. By the time I got into the office in the morning, there
were three e-mails waiting for me. Each one as magical as
the others. It's made me see what I'm missing in my life, and
how easy it would be to make it happen.

See *God, Mistaken Identity, Zero*

Phone Calls

Since I've started receiving the e-mails, I've been feeling
better. I've also had more courage about contacting John
at work. I rang him up once when I knew he was in a
meeting. I imagined his little office full of people talking
about kitchen equipment.

'I can't stop wanting you,' I said. 'Do you want me too?'

He told me yes, he believed he did.

'Would you like to make love to me now, on the carpet, with everyone looking?' I asked. He said that that would be a consideration and he would think about it very hard when it was more convenient.

'I'd take off all my clothes,' I said, 'and climb on your lap. You'd be wearing your suit but I'd be able to feel how much you wanted me through the material. I'd rub my bare skin all over you.'

He said that this was definitely a matter he needed to spend more time on. He wondered if it would be possible for us to talk about it later. When we could take it further. In more depth. Perhaps there were other angles he needed to investigate.

I put the phone down then. When we did talk about it later, he told me that he suddenly realised that he was cradling the receiver like a baby and stroking the telephone cord like it was my hair. Everyone in the room, he said, was staring at him.

He made me promise never to do it, ever again, but that night we made love for such a long time he missed his train home and had to get a taxi.

See *Codes, Marathons, Teaching, Vacuuming*

Pop Stars

Last week after we'd made love, John told me that when he was a teenager people used to think he looked like

David Bowie. He asked me which pop star I used to fancy when I was young. The phrase sounded so odd and old-fashioned coming from him like that. Pop star. Fancy. I wanted to giggle.

We were in bed. John had his eyes shut and the way he was lying against the pillow made him look as if he had a double chin, so I found a little spot on the ceiling to concentrate on instead.

Did I like David Cassidy or Donny Osmond, he asked, because in his experience girls usually went for one or the other. Although of course, he went on, his eyes still shut, if a girl was really cool she'd go for Bryan Ferry. Kate had liked . . .

By the time I turned to him, his eyes were wide open and he was watching me.

It's important to be able to talk about everything, I told him. But when I said who I'd liked when I was a teenager, he said he'd never heard of him.

I wonder if that spot on the ceiling is damp. The people above have probably let their bath water flow over. Sometimes they have no consideration. I keep watching it now every time John and I go to bed. I could swear it's getting bigger.

See *Youth*

Positive Thinking

My mother was a great believer in the power of positive thinking. Her idea of a self-help book would be called *Buck Up and Sort Yourself Out*. I tend to agree with her, so why did I spend £8.99 this lunchtime on a book called *How To Keep Your Man*? I can't stop thinking about Kate. Has she no self-respect?

See *Happiness, Impostor Syndrome*

Poverty

John says we would be very poor if we lived together. I still haven't told him about my inheritance. Instead I tell him that I know what it is to be poor.

After all, my father often told the tale about how when he was young his family didn't have enough money to buy him any clothes so he could never leave the house. But then when he was eighteen, they saved up enough money to get him a cap so he could look out of the window.

Actually, I don't think that story is true. But I do believe this one. My father's family scraped up enough money to buy him one good coat for school. They were so proud the day he went off wearing it that they all stood in the road to watch him go. But at lunchtime he didn't come back. Eventually, my grandmother went up to the school to find him and he was in the changing rooms crying because someone had stolen his brand-new coat. There was only one coat left hanging up but it was too big and very, very scruffy. Because she was so cross, my grandmother made my father wear it and his own new coat was never found.

John's grandmother used to make clothes for the gentry. One day she had to make jackets for the local hunt. She used what material was left over to make winter coats for her children, including John's mother. All the other children used to tease them but the material would never wear out because it was of such good quality. It was hunting pink.

I held John close after he told me that story. When I think of my father now, a picture of John comes into my mind. He's in a very big pink coat and he's this little shrimp, all lost and white-faced, looking out.

See *Fashion, Indecent Exposure, Objects*

Promotion

When you are happy, good things happen to you. It's all a question of attitude.

We were asked for suggestions as to how we could improve the atmosphere at work. John had just rung me up to tell me he loved me. I felt like I could rule the world.

Why not turn the downstairs store room into a staff café, I wrote. Buy in plates of sandwiches every lunchtime, put jugs of fresh orange juice on the tables, have coffee machines so people can help themselves to fresh coffee. We can talk to one another about work, relax, forge a communal atmosphere, even invite clients there.

Now everyone keeps coming up and telling me what a good idea it was. The chairman even stopped me on the stairs and asked how I was enjoying my job. Brian says I'm bound to get a promotion. I just need to keep up the good work.

John hasn't phoned me at all today. I have just spent an

hour typing out '*John call Verity. John call Verity*' over and over again. It's an attempt at mind-reading, but in reverse. A whole pile of work I'm supposed to be getting through is lying abandoned at the back of the desk. People are starting to get cross with me. Brian keeps hurrumph-hurrumphing at me from the other side of the room.

The trouble with the staff café is that I will have to spend my lunchtimes at work now. I won't be able to sneak out and meet John.

See *Bosses, Positive Thinking, Zero*

Property

I know exactly what road John and I will live in.

I walk down there regularly checking out our new neighbours. I've worked out which ones John and I will be friends with. I even plan the little dinner parties we will hold.

Once the front door of a house in the street was left open so I looked inside. All I could see was the hall, but that was painted a cheerful yellow colour which seemed a good sign.

I stood there and tried to imagine just what my life could be like, if I lived there. I could hear the low murmurs of us talking in bed at night, smell the food I would cook for John, taste his lips when I kissed him good morning, feel his suit jacket brush against my skin when he left each morning for work. In the background I could even make out other voices, children's voices, like shadows in the wind.

After a while a woman came out of the house, stared at me and slammed the door shut. I felt bereft but couldn't move. A bit later I saw her face in the bedroom window. I knew she was wondering whether to call the police. I wanted to tell her 'Don't.'

That we would be friends soon.

It was like the sun going out. Seeing that navy blue door shut out the bright yellow of mine and John's future. There was something so final about it.

See *Omens, Stalking, Utopia, Yellow*

Q

The Queen

The Queen thinks the world smells of fresh paint because everywhere she goes is freshened up especially for her.

John thinks I wear black lace underwear every day. He says it's such a change from Kate, who makes no effort.

'It's important,' I tell him, 'not to take anything for granted.'

See *Breasts, Underwear, Zest*

The Queen II

When I was sixteen, I went to Ireland with my parents on the ferry. We had just sat down to our fish and chips when a loudspeaker announcement said that the Queen was on a boat nearby and the captain would be obliged if all passengers could go up on deck to wave to her. We ran upstairs but when we got there, it was just the *Britannia* with all the sailors in white saluting at us. My mother said she could see the Queen but neither I nor my father believed her.

We had just got back to our meal, when there was another loudspeaker announcement. The Queen was really there this time, it said. We made our way up more slowly. The Queen was on a speedboat being taken back to the *Britannia* at high speed. She was dressed in a green coat and dress with a matching hat and she was standing up straight in the boat, but because it was going so fast and the sea was choppy, she waved to us so oddly she looked like a mechanical puppet.

Later my father said it was not her but a cut-out doll, but my mother told him not to be so stupid. Nevertheless, it was, my father said, a lesson in not taking things at face value.

When I asked him what he meant, he said that the Queen probably thought that our waving to her from the ferry was an outbreak of spontaneous applause because we loved her so much.

I've thought about this since. Surely no one could be that stupid.

Or could they?

See *Friends, Sex, Ultimatum, Zest*

Questions

What would you do?

John keeps asking me this. He's talking about his children. What should he do about them? I know what he wants. He wants me to make his mind up for him. But John is a Libran. If I tell him what I think, he will immediately start to see the other side. I will be in the wrong whatever I say.

I told him to divide a piece of paper into two and write down the pros and cons on each side. He came through hours later and said that the trouble was that the children mean everything to him. I felt he'd hit me.

'So do I mean nothing to you?' I asked.

'No,' he said. 'You mean everything to me too.'

And then he started to cry.

See *Horoscopes, Objects, Old, Tornados, Utopia, Vacuuming*

Quick

John has no sense of time. In this he is just like my mother. A strange thing I have noticed is that people who have no sense of time are always talking about it. They say things like 'In a minute', 'Quickly' or 'I'll get it to you soon', but the lengths of their minutes, quicklys and soons are very different from those in the rest of the world.

I can't help thinking it is deliberate. Leaving only five minutes to catch a train or bus gives the same adrenalin rush to some people as bungee jumping or walking along a high wall does to others. Whereas for most normal people being late is an inconvenience, for those like my mother and John it seems to give them a sense of power, in the same way as spending too much money, or leaving a lover's letter out where it can be read, allows people to live dangerously but within the controlled limits they have set for themselves. This way they are the architects of their own disasters.

Once I realised this I felt better about John. I tried to forgive my mother too for all the times she'd left me waiting at parties when all the other children had been picked up, but I don't think that was the same thing. I think she really did forget about me when I wasn't there.

See *Illness, Utopia*

R

Railway Stations

When you are in our position, you have to be careful in public in case anyone sees you. John and I meet in the next-door town and afterwards, I get the train home. He always walks me to the station and we shake hands. It's hard to explain but when I get on my train after that, I feel a holy glow emanating from me. I walk to my seat as if I'm some kind of prim secretary who dreams of one day letting her hands touch her boss's hair as she hands him the beautifully typed notes.

But then I sit down and think of John going back home to Kate and curse.

The other day, a couple got on just when the train doors were shutting. He was about fifty, close-cut grey hair, a business suit, the sort of boxer's face you get on men who have made it to the top the hard way. She was beautiful. In her early twenties, with honey skin and lots of long dark curls. They sat back at first, puffed out from running and giggling, but then they started to kiss. After a while, I watched his hand delve into her lap. His breath became all catchy, his eyes blurry, but then just as the whole carriage started to watch, they pulled apart. Both looked out of separate windows for a bit, but then they were drawn together again. She stood up and he lifted her by the hips to sit on his lap. All us other passengers looked at one another and smiled. It was like being in the Blitz, with their lust careering round the carriage hitting us like rifle-shot.

Eventually though, they went out into the corridor and we lost sight of them. The only way you could tell they had been there was by the briefcase and newspaper left in the luggage rack above their seats. When the train came to my station, I left by the corridor because I wanted to catch sight of them. They were pinned up against the train door, wrapped in their coats, and moving so slowly and gently it seemed they were in a dream. I thought about it all night.

The next day at the station, just as John went to shake my hand, I pulled him to me and kissed him properly.

When I got on my train and took my seat, I hoped everyone in the carriage had been watching.

See *Marathons, Toys*

Reasons . . .

. . . why Kate and John got married:

1. She was pregnant.

2. They'd known each other for years and years.

3. Their parents were good friends.

4. They liked the same food, the same books, films, music. It was easy.

5. It seemed like a good idea at the time.

6. The usual.

(Imagine that – Princess Kate pregnant before they got married!!! I tried not to look shocked for John's sake. Just a bit prim, so he'd know that this was something I'd never do. But then I got to thinking. What is the usual? What *IS* the usual? Why do people get married? Especially two people who have never really loved each other.)

See *True Romance*

Relatives

John has twenty-seven first cousins. It is difficult to imagine what it must be like to come from such a large family. I have two cousins. That is enough. Even when my mother and father were alive we didn't see much of them. My mother made sure of that. It's not surprising that we don't keep in contact now. I often think that we might meet up one day and not know each other. Blood is a funny thing.

In my magazine the other day there was an article about odd relationships. There was one woman who first met her future husband when he was eight years old and a guest at her son's birthday party. They didn't marry then, of course, but it's freaky to think she must have had her eye on him all that time. Another family were two sets of identical twins who got married. Their children therefore were genetically brother and sister even though they were really cousins.

It makes you think, doesn't it? I know for instance that your cells renew themselves after seven years, so would it be possible for your seventeen-year-old clone to marry your twenty-four-year-old self? They would be completely different people. I try to talk about all this with John, but he only starts making silly jokes. He says he has had enough of reproducing himself for ever, particularly at four o'clock in the morning when his children sometimes wake him up.

I've never really wanted to have children. I can't imagine what it must have felt like for my mother to have me squirming away inside her stomach. Like an alien.

See *Only Children, Stepmothers, Thomas the Tank Engine, Underwear*

Revenge

The chairman brings his dog into the office every day now. It sits underneath his desk and Monica has even seen it sitting in the passenger seat of the chairman's car when he goes home at night.

It turns out that the chairman's wife tried to poison it using some doctored bacon. She was jealous because the chairman spent all of his time with the dog, feeding it titbits, calling it beautiful and whispering secrets to it while fondling its ears.

We know this because the chairman's wife left a message at reception one day saying she would have felt better if the chairman had been as besotted with the bloody au pair. Brian says he bets the bloody au pair is probably a little bit more careful about what she eats in that house these days.

See *Dogs, Tornados, Vacuuming, Wobbling*

Rochester

Sally and I often talk about books.

We are searching for role models, but so far we have not found a second wife in literature who manages to keep her husband whole and healthy. We make lists of what physical deformities we would be prepared to accept – a burnt Max de Winter versus a blind Rochester. Sally says she'll take ingrown toenails as long as he isn't walletless, but I'm secretly coming to terms with the idea of a limbless, sightless and depressed John.

See *Endings, True Romance, Utopia*

Routines

There were only six months between my mother dying and my father getting ill. It wasn't a coincidence. He always had a strong will. The way he got through my mother's death was to develop a rigid pattern which held him up, even when he collapsed.

He ate the same things each day, wore particular clothes on particular days, and he devised this amazing chart which contained lots and lots of boxes which he had to tick off every half an hour. In fact, he became so busy with the chart that it was difficult for him to find the time to speak to me towards the end.

John came to see me the other day when I wasn't expecting him. I was pleased, of course, but I kept watching the television over his shoulder because my favourite programme is on a Wednesday and it had got to an exciting part.

'I thought you'd be happy to see me,' he said eventually, 'but you don't want me here.'

He was right. The funny thing was that it was only when he was getting ready to go that I realised what was happening. I asked him when he was coming next. I begged him to stay. Once he was going, I'd have done anything to get him to stay.

See *Money, Utopia, Zeitgeist*

Rude

Farting is rude. Passing wind is something that just happens.

Stealing another woman's husband is unforgivable. Falling in love is something that just happens.

Until you're old enough to start doing it, just even talking about sex is so rude it makes you giggle.

Sometimes I think John has never had sex before. He gets so excited just because I tell him we can be completely free and honest with each other. He says he thanks God for the modern woman. One night he asked me to tell him my deepest fantasy.

'I'll have to think about that,' I said. I wanted to tell him one that would make me seem daring and sexy, but not too dirty.

But then he told me his.

He said he wanted to walk down a street late at night. A few houses would still have their lights on, but there was one that didn't have the curtains drawn. He'd be able to see right in. As he walked by, he would hear the cry of 'Take me' coming from the open window. There would be an attractive couple standing there, he said, making love. The woman would see John, watch him over the man's shifting shoulder, but then the man would notice too. He'd pull out of the woman, turn and move aside. Then the woman would move over to the window and gesture for John to come inside the house. She'd not even pull her skirt down. She'd stand there, staring at John as he opened the front gate, as the man watched too. Then John would step over the threshold, unzipping himself as he did so.

He stopped talking then. He was breathing oddly, so I patted his shoulder and said it was OK, that I didn't mind. He looked a bit surprised but when we made love later, I didn't move. Just lay there on my back like a virgin. When I woke up in the middle of the night, I was curled up in a foetal position and I had a sick feeling in my stomach I didn't recognise for a while. Then I remembered. It was jealousy.

Falling in love can happen to anyone. It is very different from lusting after an unknown woman.

See *Glenda G-Spot, Jealousy, Lesbians, Vexed*

S

Sculpture

Sally has taken up lots of different hobbies so she doesn't get too preoccupied with Colin. She is studying Spanish Language, Desktop Publishing and two exercise classes at the local sports club. What she likes best though is the sculpture she studies in night school.

She's making lots of little nude figures out of clay. She makes them for Colin but of course he can't take them home so they litter their flat. She says she is making their very own orgy.

Sally told me that one of the models that came into the studio had worn a wig and how this had made all the students feel more comfortable, as if they weren't looking at a real nude body after all. Apparently they mould their pieces of clay on stands which are set up in a circle around the model and after ten minutes they move on to the next place, like a clock. You are only allowed to sculpt exactly what you see, and Sally started at the back. She says it's a big shock when she comes round to the front and realises that her sculpture has a big hole there. Although it has a perfectly formed back.

Sally thought it was a metaphor for her life. She said it was the same for me too, and that we should both think hard about what we were doing. All I could think about was what colour the model's wig was, and how I'd never really asked John whether he preferred blondes or brunettes.

See *Hair, Sex, Worst Case Scenario, Zzzz*

Sex

After she'd spent the day looking at the nude model, Sally cut off some of her pubic hair and sent it to Colin through the post so he would think of her at work. She pretends she's so independent but I can tell she's worried about him. He's not been round to the flat for a week.

She tells me she's been meeting up with the girls again, and they were talking about me.

'Let them,' I say.

'They were worried about you,' she says. 'Trust me. You can't ignore your friends. Learn from my experience if nothing else.'

I can't tell her the truth. That my experience could not be more completely different from hers if we tried.

'John's the real thing,' I point out and she touches my arm sympathetically.

'No man can be enough on his own. You have to make your own life,' she says.

I don't ask her how sending Colin perverted things like

pubic hair is being independent. But when I got home, I started thinking. Would it work with John? I thought I'd give it a go, but as soon as I cut some off, tied the hairs in red ribbon and put them in an envelope I felt so dirty I wanted to be physically sick.

Sally will never understand how different we are.

See *Friends, The Queen II, True Romance*

Sounds

There are now some nights when John can stay over with me. He tells Kate that he works at the main factory in Birmingham those days. When we lie in bed before dawn, we sometimes hear a bird outside. The bird never sings when John's not there. Then all I hear are cars, and the running footsteps of commuters, and in the distance, the sound of the station announcers and the trains going to London.

I found a list of the sounds of Earth from the *Voyager* time capsule which was sent up to space in 1977, the year I was born. I e-mailed them to John:

Whales	Footsteps and heartbeats	Horse and cart
Planets (music)	Laughter	Greetings in 54 languages
Volcanoes	Fire	Train whistle
Mud plots	Tools	Australian earthquake
Rain	Dogs, domestic	Truck
Surf	Herding sheep	Auto gears
Crickets, frogs	Blacksmith shop	Jet
Birds	Sawing	Lift-off *Saturn 5* rocket
Hyena	Tractor	A mother's kiss

Elephant	Riveter	A baby crying
Chimpanzee	Morse Code	Life signs
Wild dog	Ships	Pulse

If I were to make a record of John and me, I would include that bird singing in the morning. I'd put in the sound of him pouring boiling water into coffee mugs while I just lie in bed waiting for him to come back, the little hum John makes in his sleep, the way he laughs out loud sometimes, shocking even himself, and the gasp he makes every time I touch him down there.

See *Ears, Property, Utopia*

Stalking

Sally told me the other day that she hadn't seen Colin for a while. She said she didn't really mind because she's so busy, but it got me thinking. I hadn't walked up his road for a while so I did last night.

The lights in his house were off, and when I looked into his garden there were no toys, or swings, or anything. I think Colin must be a very cold person. Perhaps they are on holiday and he hadn't told her.

The funny thing is that it isn't that far from Colin's house to John's, but I couldn't bring myself to go down his road. I normally go later at night, when no one's on the streets and there's no chance he will see me. Once it was terrible. I was standing trying to work out which room was which, when I heard Kate come back. She was with a friend and they were laughing, holding on to each other. I had to run into their front lawn and hide in their hedge. Luckily it was pitch black. Kate kept saying what a good night she'd had and how good it had been to talk and then they'd start laughing all over again. It took her a long time to get into the house. And then when she did she started shouting that she was home. She must have woken everyone up.

I couldn't sleep that night for thinking of John and his children, waiting for Kate to come back. Their house had a very lonely atmosphere, but Kate seemed so happy. She was singing when she was looking for her keys, when she was yelling out that she was home.

See *Colin, Lesbians, Yard, Youth*

Star Quality

Brian has developed a habit of holding up his hands at cross-angles to each other and looking at me through them as if he was making a frame.

It's annoying, but of course eventually I had to ask him what he was doing. He said he thought I might be film star material. Although I'd need a lot of work on my accent to make it appealing to the ear. Flat vowels apparently don't do it for men.

I wasn't taken in. I knew from looking at his computer that he has been writing a film script. It is about a man from Yorkshire who is not appreciated by his family, but who makes friends with a little Vietnamese orphan who lives with a rich and beautiful widow in the village. This orphan is the only one to see the man's true qualities, but when the little girl introduces him to the widow, they fall in love with each other. The film ends with the three of them living out the rest of their days in luxury in a big house with a large wall around it to keep out everyone who has been scared of their 'other-ness'.

Brian leaves copies of it lying around because he wants me to ask him about it. He writes notes in the margin in large red type saying things like 'More sex?' and 'God, how true!!!'

See *Mistaken Identity, Unfit*

Startrite Sandals

John can't understand why I need so many shoes. I have just bought a pair of loafers made of turquoise leather which looks like snakeskin. I wish I could show them to Sally. They'd make her laugh too. Or they would if she could manage to stop talking about John and how I'm best rid of him for two minutes.

I still feel cheated when I buy shoes now because it's almost too easy. When I was a child it was such a procedure that they'd give us a lollipop afterwards. Just for surviving it. There was a special machine and we had to stick our feet into black boxes to have X-rays taken of how the bones were growing. It worries me how it really seemed to matter when you were a child whether you were a C or an E fitting, and now all shoes come in the same width. You just take them down from the shelf and squeeze into them somehow.

Because my feet were so wide, my mother used to make me have Startrite sandals long after everyone else had given them up. I had big feet and my shoes would flap when I walked, like a clown's. At school, the other girls would tease me and ask why I didn't just wear the shoe boxes. Or they would make rowing motions and say I was wearing boats.

I didn't have any friends at school, so I'd spend break-times posting little pebbles through the holes in the leather of my Startrites. The nuns kept coming over to make me join in other people's games, so I learnt to run round and round the playground very fast so it would look as if I was involved in a complicated game and wasn't just playing on my own.

See *Fashion, Outcast, Velvet, Vendetta*

Stationery

The only shop I would be perfectly happy to be locked in overnight is a stationery shop. After John, stationery is possibly my most favourite thing in the world. I can spend hours looking at all the different notebooks you can find, the colours of the pens, the way they feel in your hand, putting my fingers out to touch the softness of the paper, the fibres in the home-made papers, the shapes of paperclips, the solidity of staplers, sellotape dispensers, hole punchers.

I plan to myself how much better organised I would be if only I had a shelf full of home organisers, box files and see-through plastic envelopes. How I would pin up 'things to do' lists on the noticeboards, write telephone messages and personal reminders on those little sticky pads. Keep a biro on a piece of string by the telephone, so that I've always got one near and am not struggling to find one with one hand or pretending I'm writing down a complicated message when I'm not.

I think it's a female thing. John says he's never even thought about what pen he uses, just if it works. I set him a challenge one day. Just before he left me, I asked him to buy me one of those coloured pens you can get that smell of different scents – raspberry, mint, chocolate, popcorn, bubblegum. I told him just to go into the shop and ask for a smelly jelly pen. Whatever flavour he brought back, I thought to myself, would tell me what he really felt about me.

I guessed he'd forget, but he rang me up the next day. He said that when he was going into the shop in the precinct to buy me my pen, a black cat walked in with him as if they were going shopping together. He pointed this out to the shop assistant who looked up briefly and said, 'Oh not again.'

When I asked John about the pen, he said that he'd been so shaken by the cat and the man's sanguine reaction to it that he'd started looking at the cookery books on the bargain book table instead. The first one he'd picked up had a whole section about this special fruit pie his mother used to cook him. He then started telling me about his mother and what she had meant to him. He said he'd never really talked about her to anyone before.

I have noticed that John talks about himself a lot. We laugh about it sometimes, and I say 'And back to you', but it's something I can see might get annoying.

In fact, I dreamt about his mother one night soon after the pen débâcle. She was teaching me how to make banana pie with goldfishes baked through it and when we took it out of the oven together, she handed me her white apron. Interestingly, the goldfishes were still jumping up and down in the pie. I told John this but he only said that he couldn't imagine his mother sharing a kitchen with anyone, let alone the woman who broke up her son's family. I think this is just sour grapes. John has never dreamt about his mother. I think sometimes he is just not as sensitive as me. The good thing about being in love is that I can recognise John's faults in an adult fashion. I do not always want to change him.

See *Nursing, Teaching, Vexed, Women's Laughter*

Stepmothers

There was an interesting programme on the radio the other night about stepmothers. How much they can bring to a child's life, how the relationship can actually be positive because both sides get better at communicating their emotions. This is exactly what I feel. I look out of the bus sometimes and see all these mothers and daughters shopping, and think what fun they are having. I have started to keep a list of the best shops for teenagers in London. I think the important thing is not to be a mother-substitute but to be a best friend. If you think this way, there is so much you can offer a child, particularly if they look up to you and model themselves on your behaviour. The ideal stepmother is someone a child can aspire to.

See *Best Friends, Endings, Relatives, Underwear, Ultimatum*

Surnames

I told John on the telephone last night how much it mattered what surname you have. I said I'd never liked my surname. Being able to change it was one of the main reasons I wanted to get married. He laughed and said he could think of better ones.

He never takes me seriously these days.

Once he rang me from a public telephone box to tell me he'd just read about a party Oscar Wilde had hosted. He'd invited lots of strangers who couldn't think why they were there until in the middle of dinner, Oscar Wilde left the room and didn't come back. After a while, the strangers started talking and realised that what they had in common was that they all had surnames with 'bottom' in them. Longbottom, Sidebottom, Greybottom. John seemed to think this was very funny but I couldn't see the point.

It reminded me of when children at school used to boast about ringing up people in the telephone book who had silly names. I have a feeling John would do something like that. He was probably rifling through the book in the phone box looking for people with funny surnames at the same time as he was speaking to me.

I, on the other hand, was busy practising my new signature. Verity Hutchinson. I have this feeling that if I write it enough times it might just come true. I've started to underline my name now too. It makes it look much more solid.

See *Telephone Boxes, Ultimatum*

T

Teaching

I have learnt so many things since I've been with John. We stayed in a hotel together for the first time the other night, and he pointed out that I don't get out of the bath in the right way.

The funny thing is that I've never thought about it before. I've always just got out without thinking, all dripping wet, and wound myself up in towels. Sometimes I don't even bother to dry myself, just walk around like that until the water evaporates. I like the feeling of air on my skin. But this means that the bathroom is unpleasant for other people. Now I towel-dry myself standing up in the bath as the water drains out. It's a bit uncomfortable and cramped but that way I'm dry when I finally step out, and John doesn't have to step in any unpleasant damp patches.

The other thing I have learnt to do is hold my knife and fork properly. John had to point this out several times before I got the hang of it. I haven't yet managed to blink without making the little clicking noise that drives John mad, but the other night I did sleep all through the night without dribbling because I told myself again and again so many times to keep my mouth shut that I think I was still saying this when I fell asleep.

I had no idea I had so many faults. It makes me embarrassed at how I behaved in public before I met John. He is so well mannered. I tried to thank him but he just told me I was silly and that I worried too much about myself. He's right. John makes me feel large and clumsy, as if I'm always about to fall over my own feet. I have also noticed that when I am with John I tend to sweat a bit more, my nose runs and my feet sometimes have an unpleasant odour.

See *Captains, Impostor Syndrome, Zest*

Telephone Boxes (three true stories)

The telephone box that John sometimes calls me from is being pulled down because apparently more and more people are using mobile phones. I can't help feeling as if bits of our relationship are being cut off one by one. I'm scared that soon we will disappear completely so I suggested John should buy it and keep it as an historic monument, like Tom Jones did for the one he used to ring his wife from in Wales, but he just laughed. Still, it has made me think more seriously about telephone boxes. I keep finding out stories about them to tell John.

1.   An engineer was out on his rounds in a very rural part of seaside Britain when he decided to stop for his sandwich

lunch. He sat down by a telephone box perched on a cliff edge overlooking the sea. After about five minutes, the telephone started to ring so he went into the box to answer it. It was the secretary from work, who started telling him about his next job.

'How did you know I was here?' he asked.

It turned out she had dialled him on his mobile but got the wrong number. The fact that she'd reached the telephone box he'd stopped to have his lunch next to was a complete coincidence.

2. During the great storm of 1987, a man was driving to work early in the morning when he realised the hurricane was brewing. He decided to ring his wife from a telephone box to tell her to lock all the windows and doors, but as he was talking to her, the telephone box was lifted by the wind and transported into a nearby field where he found himself in the middle of a herd of cows.

The man's wife wasn't interested in this at all because she was still so cross about the fact that he'd woken her up and then hung up on her without saying goodbye.

3. My first French kiss was in a telephone box during a school dance. My favourite teacher, Mr Shepherd, pretended I had a call and then followed me into the box. I had to hold on to the sides in order to stop my knees shaking. In retrospect it wasn't the most private place to snog your teacher because of all the glass sides. When we went back into the dance, everybody started singing 'The Lord is my Shepherd'.

See *Influences, Worst Case Scenario*

Thomas the Tank Engine

John and I were in bed the other night and he rolled me over on top of him and lifted me up and down.

'Chuff, chuff,' he said. 'This is hard work for the Fat Controller.'

I wish he wouldn't bring his children into everything.

See *Toys*

Thrush

Recently when I have been going to the loo, I have noticed a smell like freshly baked bread. I thought it was because I was getting ready to settle down. That I was finally becoming domesticated. It made me feel like nesting.

But then John told me that he wondered whether I was infecting him. He said he'd been too embarrassed to tell me before but that he'd developed a rash which came up after we made love. I went to the doctor and even though it was quickly cleared up, it was still possibly the worst thing I've ever had to do. And then to cap it all, John was cross with me. He said he didn't know how he was going to bring the subject up with Kate.

I felt so guilty, I said I was sorry. But of course he doesn't need to tell her anything. They haven't had any relations like that for a long time.

See *Friends, Horror Movies, Old, Reasons, Rude*

Tornados

John was supposed to be spending Sunday with me, but Kate was ill so he had to take his children to the Natural History Museum. I was so cross about this that he bought me a pet tornado from the shop there as a joke.

It's just a little plastic tube filled with water and glitter, but if you turn it quickly backwards and forwards, you can watch your own little twister develop. John and I can't stop playing with it. He says other people can keep their dogs, we have a tornado. He even got a book about them for me so we could find out more.

He's taken to calling me F-5 as a nickname. This level of tornado reaches wind speeds of more than 300 miles per hour. The devastation is total. It causes homes to disintegrate, foundations to be left bare, posessions scattered. It has been known to wreak considerable damage even to steel-reinforced structures.

When John's not there, I hide the tornado in a drawer. It upsets me.

See *Dogs, Names, Revenge, Vacuuming*

Toys

Apparently vibrators have been around much longer than you would imagine. They were invented by doctors who were bored with men bringing their hysterical wives to them for treatment. To begin with, the doctors used to relieve the women by bringing them to climax manually but then someone had the clever idea of inventing a machine to do the same job.

Much less messy and healthier all round. How those men must have congratulated themselves. They didn't realise what they had unleashed.

Monica asked me whether I remembered Jean from the sex party and I couldn't think who she meant until she called her Cathy Come.

Apparently at the party Cathy had bought some of those little balls you put up yourself and decided to wear them the next time she went to the supermarket. It was fine at first, rather nice and tingly, but then the sensation got worse and by the time she got to frozen foods, Cathy couldn't stop coming. Eventually, she had to abandon her shopping at the checkout and try to walk home. She'd only got about a hundred yards when she found herself clinging to a lamp-post, unable to move without groaning.

The funny thing was that no one who walked past her gave her a second look. She had become invisible.

See *Codes, Glenda G-Spot, Glitter, Weight*

True Romance

I have just remembered one of my mother's stories. At the time I thought it was a disgusting tale and couldn't think why she'd told it. Who wanted to hear about old people in love?

My mother said she'd heard about a woman who had been married for forty years. Her husband loved her almost obsessively and they had one of those particularly close relationships you're supposed to get with couples who don't have children.

But this woman had a secret. When she was younger and first married, she had fallen in love with an architect. He begged her to leave her husband and move in with him, but she refused. The couple tried many times to leave each other but they were always drawn back – sometimes by an argument, sometimes by a smell, a memory that made it impossible not to get in contact, sometimes by a bit of good or bad luck that they could only share with each other. Eventually, they came to the conclusion that their connection was stronger than them. That to sever this would be at the cost of cutting out a bit of themselves that would make it impossible to live.

However, the architect realised that if he forced the woman to leave her husband she would come to him as a different person. All the soft edges he loved about her would have to be sawn off in order for her to survive the rift. She would have to want to come to him, leaving none of her heart with her husband. In the meantime, the lovers agreed that they would meet once a year and share a weekend of romance.

After five years, the couple were still as much in love with each other as they ever had been. They shyly admitted that these weekends had become the centre of their lives, but the last night was always spent with the woman in tears. How could she leave her husband? He needed her.

The architect decided to spend the next year praying for a solution. After a few months, he felt a stirring within. One night he woke up and in half sleep made his way to his drawing board. The lines he made on the plain paper were not coming from his brain, but direct from his heart.

When the couple met up, he was ready. It was with a tender proudness, a certainty, that he unrolled the drawings he had tucked under his arm. He took her hand and traced the rooms, the lightness of the proportions, the sheer originality of the house spread in front of them, with her fingers. It was his hopes for the future he was parading in front of her. How could he fail?

When the woman returned to her husband two days later, the architect sat alone and studied the abandoned drawings. The lines blurred with his tears and he suddenly saw how he had gone wrong. How hopeless this shape had been, the clumsiness of the end wings meant it would never take flight. This was not the house she could ever want to live in with him. How right she had been. How right she always was. He found a pencil and started work again immediately.

Each year, the architect would design another house for his love to live in with him. She never came, but he didn't stop planning either. Sometimes a couple would come to his studio in order to have a house designed for them. The wife would get bored with discussions about budgets and work schedules and start to flick through the architect's plans. Always, he noticed, it would be the drawings for his love which would capture the wife's attention. There was something about them that called to the woman's heart. Once, one wife had even pulled out a plan. Had called her husband over. Had demanded that the architect design something just like this for them too. Something as romantic.

He refused, even when the couple threatened to leave and find another, more malleable architect. He realised something, however, that night as he pored over the drawings and wondered what it was that attracted the strange woman so much, but not the one he had intended this house for. He realised that all the years of giving his heart on paper had had an effect. Somewhere along the line he'd given up hope without realising it. The drawings were without teeth now. They were pretty enough to attract those that had everything but were not daring or brave enough to be worth real risk and sacrifice.

He kept going though. The only difference was that his drawings became more fanciful. Less believable. The woman seemed to appreciate them more. She exclaimed over tree houses, perched high in the sky. Laughed over underground tunnels, as comfortable and as traditional as a badger's set.

He took her praise, her love, for what it was and tried to make it enough. Only after she'd gone would he go back into his studio and weep over the houses he'd dragged out from somewhere deep within his body. The maps of his heart. All leading back to nowhere.

My mother had laughed after she'd told this story, but my father looked sad. He'd taken her hand and circled the centre of her palm with his fingers. I remember feeling strangely angry. Why did I feel cold when I was with them, as if I was sitting in their shadow? It was partly to warm myself up that I told them how I wanted to find someone to love me like that architect. I wanted to be adored that much. My father looked at me as if he wasn't seeing me at first. Then he got angry. He said, couldn't I understand anything? That the real love in the story was between the husband and wife.

See *Endings, Illness, Utopia*

U

Ultimatum

Sally has got so tough from all this independence business that she thought it would be a good idea to tell Colin that unless he left his wife for her, she would leave him.

I could have told her this was a bad idea, but the situation is even worse than I suspected. Colin's divorce actually came through six months ago. His ex-wife has been happily living in Wolverhampton with a dental technician all this time.

I can't blame Sally for refusing to have anything else to do with Colin, even though he says he was going to tell her. He just hadn't found the right moment. The trouble is that now Colin agrees with Sally that she has to leave the flat straight away. It seems he was cleverer than her because he'd only taken out a short-term lease whereas Sally's lodgers have got six more months in her own flat before she can get rid of them.

Still, Colin says Sally mustn't give him any second

chances. He doesn't deserve them. Sally has devoted herself to him for too long.

A situation like this is particularly hard because it isn't just a romantic liaison for Sally, it's like giving in your notice at work too.

See *Ambition, Colin, Endings, Worst Case Scenario, Yields*

Underwear

My mother took Sally and me together to buy our first bras. Afterwards she took us to the coffee shop as a treat and let us choose whichever cake we wanted. She watched us eat them, the cream oozing between our fingers, while she smoked. In my memories, my mother always seemed to be circled with cigarette smoke as if she was already fading away.

Sally couldn't wait to get to school to show her bra off, but mine felt itchy and uncomfortable. It was like that first week back to school in the autumn, when you crammed your feet into shoes after a summer wearing open sandals. The leather was so creaky, pinch-tight and solid all around your sole, constantly reminding you of timetables and rules.

It's become a habit of Sally's and mine now to buy our underwear together. Whereas once we used to feel more successful the more material we needed for our bras, now we spend a month's salary on garments designed to look as if we're wearing nothing.

The last time we went, Sally and I got the same set – purple silk with a silver ribbon woven through the edges.

Sally said we looked like strippers. We were just walking over to the café to have our cream cakes when Sally suddenly turned to me and said, 'I loved your mother.' I was so surprised I nearly walked straight into the road, but then we couldn't stop laughing, because we were both wearing the sort of lingerie that makes you long to be run over by a bus so you can make the ambulance man's day. Just like our mothers always told us.

See *Breasts, Moustache, The Queen, Velvet, Zzzz*

Unfit

Several clients have complained about Brian's unreliability so he was called in to see the managing director yesterday to be given an official warning. I have never seen anyone as angry as he was when he came out of that office. We all pretended to be busy with our work, trying not to catch his eye, but Brian was like one of those magnets attracting iron filings. All the hairs on his arms and even his beard seemed to be standing up, spiking out from him, forming a dark shadow.

He just sat at his desk staring at the same piece of paper. At lunchtime I asked whether he wanted me to get him a sandwich, but he shook his head.

'Are you sure? You have to eat, you know.'

He looked up. 'Do I?' he said. The funny thing is that Brian has quite a nice face when he hasn't been drinking.

'There's always your film,' I said. I was trying to make things better.

'Christ, Verity, grow up, can't you?' he said. 'This isn't

a game, you know.' Then he stormed out and didn't come back for the rest of the afternoon.

We worked in silence until it was time to go home. It was as if all the air had been sucked out of the office.

See *Indecent Exposure, Star Quality, Wobbling*

Utopia

I've noticed that the way John talks about the time when he leaves Kate and we live together has changed.

It is now much more if-only-ish. And wonderful too. It seems that when John and I get together, we're going to be surrounded by light and sun and birds singing and fairies fluttering and mermaids mer-ing.

I don't know why but I felt more comfortable when he was glooming around, saying how unhappy we were going to be. At least that was realistic.

I suppose I should be looking for some way to get John's feet back on the ground, but I'm worried about Brian. He hasn't been in the office for two days. I've been covering for him with clients, and have even managed to do some of the writing myself. Not even the managing director has noticed and although I'm not sure how long I can do this, I feel a responsibility towards Brian.

See *Marathons, True Romance, Unfit, Yellow*

V

Vacuuming

John is much tidier than me. Sometimes he will come back
to my flat after work and before he even takes off his
jacket, he starts cleaning up. I try not to say anything, but
it drives me mad. He says it relaxes him but I can't help
thinking it's an insult. And boring.

The other day he took out the vacuum cleaner and
started doing the sitting-room floor. He kept having to
bend down to pick things up, and after a while I noticed
that he was still crouched on the floor even though the
machine was still on.

I asked if he was all right. He lifted his head then, and
his face looked as if he was bruised under the eyes.

He told me that at home when he did this, his dog would
always attack the hoover. That he and it had fights that they
both looked forward to. He said it seemed soulless, hoovering just backwards and forwards on his own.

I didn't know what to say. I had expected John to be

upset about the children. But animals? John knows I am allergic to them. At his family home he has a dog, two guinea pigs, a rabbit, a three-legged cat and two goldfish. I've noticed he has this maternal streak. He even pats our tornado in passing. I wonder how Kate puts up with it. It must be like living in a zoo.

See *Dogs, Kitchen Equipment, Sex, Stationery, Tornados, Utopia*

Velvet

In my pocket, I keep a corner cut out from the velvet curtains that hang in the spare room of Sally's parents' house. Because I took it from the hem so no one would notice, it's a rich red and not the faded tea-stained colour of the rest of the curtains.

I run my thumbnail along the fabric when I get upset. It can go surprisingly deep and when I rub against the grain I get a feeling not unlike when you put your tongue on the metal bit of a pencil sharpener. It's almost an electric shock but softer. I like it because it reminds me that there are other worlds out there. It's a world Sally must have running through her veins.

See *Fashion, Houses, Magazines, Money, Utopia, Zzzz*

Vendetta

It is strange to think that someone could actually hate me as much as Kate would do if she found out who I was.

Hate is such an active emotion. I talked to Sally about it and she said, rather too casually, that people hated me at school. I was shocked. I knew they'd rather not play with me, but to hate me? That was something different. I couldn't think what I'd done to deserve that.

'It was your big eyes,' she said, 'and your hair. You were always staring at people as if you wanted to get inside them somehow. We used to think you were a witch.'

I remembered the time Sally had caught me making up that rain-dance. It was just something I'd seen on television, but now I was surprised at how much I liked this image of myself.

'My mother was a witch,' I lied, thinking Sally would laugh at me.

'They say it's inherited. Your mother was magic,' she said, and carried on reading the television guide. Sally is always round my house these days. While we were watching a film later on, I willed and willed her to go. As soon as the film finished, she picked up her bag and left.

'It's all right,' she said. 'I'm going.' Although I hadn't said anything.

I couldn't wait to get to work the next day to try something similar out on Brian, but he kept catching my eye when I was staring at him and winking back at me.

See *Bosses, Mistaken Identity, Names, Voices, X-ray Vision*

Vexed

John's nickname for me is Squiggle. When I write to him now, I sign it Sxxx. He says it makes him think of sex.

Recently there have been times when I've wondered if this is all he thinks about. I can't help being shocked by how much it is starting to bore me. I asked him the other day, for instance, if he missed me.

'Yes,' he said. 'I was feeling really randy this morning. I could have done with you then.'

I wrote a note to Brian and signed it Vx by mistake. He looked up immediately of course and smiled. I had to smile back and although I wanted to tell him he was wrong, I wasn't really sending him kisses, he looked so happy I couldn't.

See *Breasts, Ice Cream, Memory, Outcast, Phone Calls, Rude, Teaching*

Victim

I'm very busy now, particularly as Brian has been giving me work as a thank you for helping him out. I've been working on a new customer magazine for a company that makes industrial-sized pipes for construction companies. I came up with the title *In the Pipeline* which Brian likes a lot. He says if the project goes well, he is going to recommend I get promoted officially to be his assistant on this newsletter, with more to come. John wasn't as pleased as I would have

liked. He thinks that Brian probably has hidden mo-
tives, but I don't think this is a very supportive
attitude. John did apologise. He said that he is so
frantic at work too, it just seems a shame that I can't
be free in the little time he has to see me.

I tried to see his point. He has had to put up with being
second best with Kate and the children for such a long
time now. He can't bear for it to happen all over again.

See *Ambition, The Queen, Stationery, Utopia*

Visible

The hairdresser kept asking if I was sure. Eventually I just
shut my eyes so we couldn't keep looking at each other in
the mirror. I could hear how people kept coming over to
watch her, picking up curls from the floor and telling me
how different I would feel when it was done.

'A new person,' they said.

Hair as thick as mine makes a remarkable noise when
it's being cut, like a knife sawing through bones. It got
louder and louder the more she cut, until I thought I was
going to have to tell her to stop. I suppose it was because I
had no protection over my ears now.

At the end I told her it looked lovely, that I was
delighted, but she wouldn't stop showing me the back
of my neck in the mirror. She obviously didn't believe
me, but she was wrong. I do love it.

I dreaded going into work the next day though. I knew
people wouldn't know what to say. It was the same when
my parents died. Reactions were divided into two camps.

Some people ignored the fact that anything had happened, while others wanted to know every last detail. I started to feel as if my loss was filling a hunger in them and that they would eat me up if they could. As if all these bad things happening to me spared them.

I could see my haircut worried everyone. Even as they were telling me how nice I looked, most were putting their hands up their necks, checking that their hair was still there, that they were all right, that my misery hadn't leapt over to them. Like fleas.

See *Codes, Hair, Objects, Weight*

Voices

Now that our telephone box has finally been pulled down, I am on a mission to keep others going for lovers everywhere. Every time I see one, I go in and ring someone up, although it can sometimes surprise them. Recently, I've been ringing the number of my mother and father's house. It's been disconnected, and of course I know she won't, but I can't get rid of this hope that my mother will answer. I'm scared I'll forget what her voice sounded like. If I shut my eyes, I hear it very loud and screechy saying things like 'No one's impressed by your misery, you know.' But then I try to listen with Sally's ears and it's different. It's not my father talking any more, interpreting my mother for me. I know there's a saying that you turn into your mother as you get older. Maybe everyone's the same. We're all trying to listen harder and harder to – not just the words – but what our mothers were really saying to us all those years ago.

See *Codes, Daisies, Doors, Elephant's Egg, Telephone Boxes, Underwear, Vendetta, Washing Powder*

Voyeur

Sally and I spent last Saturday shopping for old times' sake. However, she didn't have any money, and I could think of nothing I wanted to buy, so we just walked round in silence. Eventually she had the idea that we should each buy the other a tattoo.

'What would you have?' I asked and she said that she would have SALLY tattooed on her arm in beautiful rainbow colours, in case she forgot who she was.

'And me?' I asked.

'You'd have SALLY too, of course,' she said. But then because I looked so worried, she bought me a pair of novelty rainbow earrings made out of telephone wire instead.

I went to the loo to try them on when we went for coffee. I was in such a rush that I must have forgotten to shut the door because just as I was putting the second one in I looked up and saw a man standing in the doorway watching me through the mirror. He wasn't attractive, just an ordinary middle-aged, tired-looking businessman but he was watching me with such intensity I felt we'd both been caught doing something far too intimate. He was just staring at me, running his fingers round his shirt collar, when our eyes locked and my whole body turned to liquid. I don't know how long we stood there, we couldn't seem to look away, but suddenly I froze, shut my eyes, and when I looked up, he'd gone. He'd even shut the door.

By the time I rejoined Sally, I was ready to shop. Only buying enough solid things would fill the gap that man had left in me. I didn't tell Sally. She thought I was relaxing at last and took advantage by picking out clothes she knew I would never normally wear but which went with my new hairstyle. A fresh start, she kept saying. I even dragged her into the changing rooms with me. It wasn't just because we were having so much fun. I didn't want to be left alone with the mirror again.

See *Breasts, Indecent Exposure, Railway Stations, Wrists*

W

Washing Powder

John hasn't been free to see me at the weekends for a long time now. There are times when I don't speak to anyone from the time I leave work on Friday to when I get back to the office on Monday morning. I have got so lonely, I have been known to ring the speaking clock just to hear the sound of someone else's voice. But last week I had a bit too much to drink. On an impulse, I phoned the helpline advertised on the side of the washing-powder box. The lady who answered was really friendly. And Scottish. I told her how I'd read somewhere that they employed Scottish people because they sounded more like human beings but she said it was because they were cheaper and we laughed. We really did laugh together. Like friends do.

She asked me what machine I was using, and I said it was me that needed help. I told her how what I wanted most in the world was to be held. No one had held me for such a long time. I wanted to be hugged and washed and cleansed until I was white all over. That's when she told me I should call the Samaritans. I laughed and said they were just for unhappy people. Didn't she realise she was talking to someone who was so evolved she'd once spent a week writing her obituary in order to guarantee happiness?

It was then she said she was going to have to call her supervisor. There was no need for her to do that.

See *Friends, Happiness, Phantom E-mails, Wobbling, Yard*

Weight

Sometimes I don't think my body can bear the weight of the pain that is being inflicted on it.

I've started to go to the gym just to build myself up. I want to be strong so that no one can push me around ever again. I want to weigh myself down so my feet stay on the ground. I want to become such a presence that everyone can see me. I don't ever want to become invisible.

Most of all I want to matter.

See *Boxing, Codes, Gwyneth Paltrow, Kindness, Stepmothers, Youth*

What If . . .

– you could win a competition to be Queen for a year?
– it was a crime to have money?
– you woke up one morning and everyone was speaking a different language?

– there really were tiny little people living and working inside those machines, printing your passport photos, counting out your cash and making your coffee?
– children never grew up?
– you lived your life backwards?
– you could make time stand still?
– rich women went on a shopping strike?
– people stopped dying?
– John really had left Kate and married me?

See *Endings, Friends, True Romance, Utopia, Zest*

Why?

Sally has agreed to listen to me talk about John on Friday evenings and Sunday lunchtimes, but only if I will cook for her. She says it's too much to cope with on an empty stomach.

I stand at the oven stirring, while the tears run down my cheeks, and I press the bruise again and again. I go over every detail of our relationship – how we met, how John looked when he first kissed me, how I knew we were meant for each other, the connection we felt between us and how I can't bear it that it is broken. Sometimes Sally will lean across and taste what I'm cooking, but mostly she'll just nod along. The funny thing is that she really does listen.

The other day I turned to her and I could only think of the one word to say. 'Why?' I shouted it out.

She looked a bit frightened which, despite my pain, made me want to laugh. 'Why what?' she asked.

'Why wasn't I good enough for him?' I said. 'Why didn't he want me?'

She shook her head. 'You gave him up, Verity,' she said. 'It was you who finished it.'

I sat down. I couldn't finish cooking the meal. I know I told John to go but I didn't mean it. Surely Sally of all people could understand that. I suddenly saw that what had happened to me was exactly the same as with Colin and her. And all I'd wanted to do was to prove how different we were.

It was then that I decided to stop talking about John. He is now a closed book.

See *Endings*, *The Queen II*, *Sex*, *Ultimatum*, *Zeitgeist*

Withdrawal

I read somewhere that in some parts of Japan, mothers breastfeed their babies for longer than we do in this country because they want to give their children the best possible start.

But when they decide enough is enough, they don't wean them off gently. One morning they paint their breasts with terrifying and horrific pictures and then wake the children up softly to take the breast just as before. The children are so filled with fright they never want to feed from their mothers again.

This way, it is the child who has given up the breast and honour is satisfied on both sides.

See *Horror Movies*, *Ultimatum*, *Voices*

Wobbling

The chairman has been on lots of courses aimed at positivity. If you ask him how he is these days, he no longer tells you he is surviving and starts patting his dog. Instead, he looks you in the eye and says he's fan-tas-tic, or that everything is simply wonderful.

He has even taken to putting little quotes up at reception to buoy us up each day. Most people scoff at these, but Brian and I have become secretly addicted. We have taken to getting to work earlier and earlier just to see what today's quote will be. I think we're both looking for a message that will give us the clues we need to join the rest of the human race. We want to be winners too.

The other day I came in to find Brian had taped something to my computer. *Even if you are falling flat on your face, you are still moving forward*, I read.

Brian has been surprisingly kind to me. It is funny how it takes something dreadful happening to you to find out who your real friends are.

See *Codes, Dogs, God, Positive Thinking, Voices, Weight*

Women's Laughter

The only time I ever saw my father get angry with my mother was once when she was helpless with laughter on the telephone. He practically ran across the room, pulled the receiver from her hand and slammed it down.

She just looked at him and laughed even louder, until

he slapped her. He told me afterwards that he didn't do it to hurt Mummy but to stop her getting hysterical.

I understood what he was saying at the time, but probably even better now. Women's laughter is different from any other kind of laughter. It is louder, more generous, more absorbing and all-encompassing. It is as if they have forgotten other people exist. While women are laughing, they don't care about anybody else but each other. If someone else tries to join in, the laughter dries up immediately and the women bustle round getting busy with one of the hundreds of jobs they always seem to have to do.

I have a sneaking suspicion that if women laughed less, men might be happier.

See *Danger, Friends, Impostor Syndrome, Lesbians, Stalking, Victim*

Woolworth's

After the success of our last shopping expedition, Sally and I now spend Saturdays shopping in town. Last weekend she said she wanted to take me out for a special treat, and then took me to Woolworth's. I was surprised. When we were kids, during the summer holidays, we used to pretend to our mothers we were just going to the park near our estate, but then we'd jump on a bus and have baked beans on toast in the Woolworth's in the centre of town.

For pudding, we'd steal sweets from the 'Pick'n'Mix' counter. We weren't the only ones. Even nowadays you get adults looking at the sweets in Woolworth's with a nostalgic look on their face. They buy selections for their own children, but you can tell they think there's something unenterprising about this. Something unnatural about just handing over the money, but then children these days expect everything to fall on their plates without doing any of the work, don't they?

I was about to point this out to Sally, when I saw her face. 'I want you to get me a candy shrimp, a fruit chew, two pear drops and a coconut mushroom,' Sally said. For a few seconds I thought about refusing but there would be no point. I know Sally too well.

We ran down the street afterwards, whooping and shrieking with joy. My hands were sweating so much that most of the sweets had disintegrated but I didn't care. I kept looking into the faces of everyone passing me by, and just at that moment, it was as if Sally and I were the only ones who were truly alive.

See *Codes, Danger, Kindness, Women's Laughter, Zzzz*

Words

Sometimes when I have a lot of work to type, I get confused over words. They start to look odd. I told Brian about this and he agreed. We made a list of silly words together. 'Eighth', for instance, is completely ridiculous once you analyse it. So is 'put'. Almost an insult.

We tried to write a letter together using every word on our list, but had to give it up we were laughing so much.

'You're all right sometimes, Ver,' he said, which surprised me because he didn't then go on to make a joke about it. He's changed a lot since his warning. These days he's more like an unbounced Tigger. More manageable. He says the same about me.

What I didn't say to Brian – because he'd only get the wrong idea – is that one of the strangest words is 'husband'. You can't help but break it into two syllables in your mouth. 'Hus' is like a snake caught between your tongue and the top edge of your teeth. It makes your lips sneer to say it. And then 'Band' is almost dismissive. Draws your mouth back and lets any passion out without there being anything you can do about it. Say it carefully enough and your lips are in exactly the right position to have a gag tied around so you can't utter another word.

This is something I wish I'd never discovered, because now I can't stop thinking about it.

See other silly words in this Lexicon *Ants, Ears, Gwyneth Paltrow, Lesbians, Noddy, Rude, Thrush, Ultimatum, Vendetta, Zen*

Worst Case Scenario

Brian says it's one step forward, two steps back. As soon as he's got his work situation sorted out, his home life has gone to pot. It turns out his wife has only been putting up with him because she thought he'd collapse without her, but now she says he doesn't need her any more. He said the funny thing is that he's been fearing this moment for such a long time, his first feeling was one of complete relief. It's as if he can start again.

I think of Sally. She says she will never trust another man again. She says that she doesn't need a man any more. She says she is perfectly happy just being on her own. She says that she has saved up enough money from the time she was living off Colin so that she will never have to be dependent on anyone else ever again. She even says Colin has done her a favour.

It's humbling to think that the worst thing anyone can imagine is probably happening to someone, to some family, somewhere in the world right now. You can never be complacent. You can never just let things go on day after day without taking action, like Brian says he did.

See *Illness, Old, Utopia, Withdrawal*

Wrists

The other day on the tube there was a man standing up in front of me. He was holding on to the strap and reading his newspaper. I was just looking at the headlines but then his wrist caught my attention.

I couldn't stop staring.

His wrist was beautiful. There is something about certain men's wrists just poking out of a jacket sleeve that gets me every time. That little nobble on the edge of his bone and the hollow in the middle of the flat bit that joins hand and arm. It's impossible to see a man with a wrist like that and not think of what he could do to you with his fingers.

I kept thinking what bit of my body had the same effect

on John. It sounds strange but I liked the backs of his knees best. It was as if no one else had ever touched them but me. Sally has beautiful ears. When she's busy talking sometimes, she twists her hair behind her ears and she looks like a little puppy dog. Her face is so sweet and vulnerable I want to crush her to me. It's hard to explain, that mixture of wanting to hurt and wanting to care for someone all at the same time.

I was pleased when my station came and I could get off.

See *Danger, Elephant's Egg, Nostrils, Railway Stations, Velvet*

X

Xenophobia

My father hated going abroad. When my mother did manage to persuade him to go on a foreign holiday, he'd never be happier than when he found a view or a street that reminded him of the Home Counties.

'You could almost be in England,' he'd say in admiration and he would look around as if he'd found something remarkable. It used to drive my mother mad – the fact that he really did think that it was this that made coming abroad worthwhile.

Sally and I have been planning lots of foreign holidays together. I phoned my solicitor to see how much money I had.

'Verity, your investments are so sound you could practically buy the airline,' he said, and when I started to say that I didn't really think I wanted to go that far, he interrupted to say he'd been joking.

'You really must take an interest,' he said. 'This is your future security we're talking about.'

I pretended he was right, because I knew he'd only give me a lecture otherwise. I said that I'd start to read the business pages and get actively involved.

I even asked whether he'd help me understand it all a little better. He went all huffy and puffy and said he'd be delighted. He said that, even if he said it himself, he'd been doing something rather clever and exciting with my capital investments which he thought I'd find rather amusing.

I told him I couldn't wait.

See *Ambition, Codes, Houses, Illness, Promotion, Voices, Yields*

X-rated

Colin rang me up at work. I was surprised but thought he'd called about Sally. I was all set to be a good best friend and put him straight about a thing or two, when he suddenly asked me if I wanted to have an affair with him.

I couldn't think of anything to say. Eventually I said I was sorry.

'No harm in asking,' he said and rang off.

I phoned Sally straight away. I thought this was something she ought to know and I'd rather she heard it from me than anyone else. I was surprised when she burst out laughing.

She said she'd been expecting something like this, just never thought it would happen so quickly. It was relief that made her laugh, she said. Relief that she didn't feel sadder about it. Sometimes you need to go as near to the edge as you can, for all the bad things you're imagining to pile up one on top of each other, so you can stop wondering about what might have happened. You know the worst.

'Typical Colin though,' she said then. 'He's always had fantasies about the two of us, you and me.'

When I put the phone down, I realised that Sally had painted a very different picture of what happened from what I think Colin was actually intending, but I suppose she's just trying to protect herself.

I had a long bath that night. Even if Sally was wrong, I wanted to wash off the feeling of being part of someone else's porn movie.

See *Colin, Lesbians, Phantom E-mails, Rude, Voyeur, Youth*

X-ray Vision

Sally could be right about the fact that I have special powers. It's not something I like to talk about, but I am peculiarly sensitive to what people are really thinking. Gifts like this have to be used responsibly. Not everyone wants someone else looking inside their brain.

I have started to practise it with John. I sit cross-legged on the ground, hold a piece of his writing in between my hands and then I just concentrate.

I know when I connect with John because I feel this rush of energy surge through me and I get this picture in my mind like I'm this tiny little figure throwing herself on top of John and just clinging there. It does worry me that it always feels like this. As if I'm one of those monkey dolls hanging round a child's neck and not letting go.

I have to peel myself off before I can start to transmit thoughts to John. I tried it with Colin the other day. I thought of him replacing the receiver after I'd turned him down and saw how upset he was. The interesting thing was that Colin and I were walking hand-in-hand through a field of shining buttercups. I didn't do that clinging thing, and I was able to transmit to Colin easily. I felt he needed me so I sent him healing thoughts.

Sometimes now when I use my powers I'm not sure who is going to pop up – John or Colin. I don't do it so often any more.

See *Omens, Sculpture, Teaching, Vendetta, Zest*

X

There are things about Sally nowadays that keep reminding me of my mother. For instance, I had forgotten how strongly my mother believed in education. She was always attending classes at the local adult education centre too. It was almost a religion with her. She'd search through the brochure every autumn, working out what to do. It was an interesting way to gain knowledge because she became an expert on specialist subjects such as Stonehenge, garden history and the Greek tragedies, but was unable to add up a single row of figures. It was as if she was in training to become the perfect quiz contestant.

I found my grandparents' wedding certificate in my mother's drawer after she died. I was thinking about framing it when I noticed that my grandmother's father had signed with an X. I suddenly thought about my mother sitting at the kitchen table struggling over her books, and I felt so ashamed about how annoyed I was at the time because she was taking up so much space. I can't help wondering now what it must have been like in her house when she was growing up. Did they read books? How did she get to love reading so much? Is this why she was always buying books for me to read? I'd forgotten how many books she used to buy me, how we used to go to the library together every week.

If God had had a family, he'd have created a telephone number you could use for all those questions you need to ask dead people once it's too late. A mobile with wings.

See *Telephone Boxes, Voices*

Y

Yard

The other night, I found myself walking down Colin's road. This is not because he interests me. It has become a habit from when he first took up with Sally.

I was surprised to see a milk bottle that had been painted gold left out in the empty yard next door to Colin's house. I couldn't imagine who had done such a thing, or why.

I often see incidents like this. It's as if I am more aware of what is going on around me than other people. The other day, for instance, I saw a couple going round a music shop filling up a basket each with CDs. Why was that? Had they won the lottery? Or maybe they were both starting music collections from scratch?

And then there was the old man on the train who was composing a complicated musical score on the back of a business letter. The businessman carrying a school satchel.

The middle-aged woman taking a rabbit for a walk in the park with a collar and lead.

It's hard when the stories queue up like this and there's no one to tell them to. I thought I might call Colin and tell him about the milk bottle. It seems only polite since he contacted me so recently and it was in his neighbour's yard. I thought he might be interested.

See *Doors, Endings, Foreheads, Phantom E-mails, Stalking, X-ray Vision*

Yellow

I have spent the weekend painting my hallway a cheerful yellow. It was exhausting, but I have rarely felt so satisfied as when I finished. I kept going outside into the street so I could open my front door and see how good it looked.

I told Brian about it on Monday and he said I'd created my own little sunlit island. I rushed home from work just so I could see it again. I even left the door on the latch so people walking past could glimpse in and feel jealous of me and my home.

See *Doors, Property, Sculpture, Utopia, Washing Powder, Wobbling*

Yields

Sally came round for supper to see my painting. I noticed that the conversation kept turning towards Colin and that

I blushed every time she mentioned his name, so I tried to change the subject.

We started talking about Brian, and all our other friends with disastrous love-lives, but then we got back to Colin again, so I asked Sally about her investments instead. She has decided to keep her flat rented out, and to buy another flat to live in. I was interested in this, because I'd been reading the papers like I promised the solicitor and there'd been several articles recently about the buy-to-let market in the suburbs. The solicitor keeps telling me that the yields we've been getting on my parents' house are disappointing, and although the tenants are safe, he wonders if I need to maximise my investments.

I thought about the last meeting I'd had with the solicitor, and tried to practise some of the language I'd learnt on Sally.

'It could be an idea,' I told her, 'to buy some property for short-term lets for all the people who have to move somewhere quickly when their relationships have broken down.'

But then we couldn't stop talking. We planned out a hostel for the broken-hearted, with sound-proofed rooms so you could cry without anyone hearing you, enormous soft sofas to sink into, comfort food delivered to your door, country music piped into your bedroom, plastic bricks to throw at walls, and lots and lots of shoulders to lean on.

'Just like the song,' she said. I could tell she thought it was just a bit of fun, but when she'd gone home I started making notes. In the morning, I rang the solicitor and told him my mother's story about the architect and his lover. He said it sounded very interesting and made an appointment for me to come and see him to talk more about it.

See *Codes, Houses, Money, True Romance, Xenophobia, Youth*

You

I knew I shouldn't have done it. I knew it was a mistake even as I was dialling the number, but some time ago I had written myself a note in my diary that today I could call John. Since then, I've been counting off the days. There were times when it was all that kept me going. However, even when I was waiting for him to answer I was telling myself I'd never do it again. And then when he answered the phone and said 'Hello, you,' I could tell he didn't know who it was for a second. He said he was pleased to hear from me and that he missed me, but I kept thinking about the way he'd said 'Hello, you,' and how different it was from every time he'd said it before.

When I put the phone down, I wrote another note in my diary for when I could call him again, but this is for a long time in the future. Anything could happen before then.

See *Grief, Mistaken Identity, Phonecalls, Why?*

Youth

Brian read out a bit from the newspaper which said that men were genetically programmed to fall in love for a final but lasting time when they reach the age of fifty-one. What is interesting about this is that when John is fifty-one, I will be thirty-nine, and apparently women of that age are often at their most fertile. This was the first thing I thought of, even though I haven't spoken to John for a while. Still, it is nice to know we have fourteen more years before nature is ready for us if something should happen.

I eventually plucked up enough courage to call Colin. He couldn't work out who I was at first, but then he suddenly burst out laughing.

'Verity,' he said, as if I hadn't just been repeating my name. 'Sally's desperate friend.'

I couldn't believe it. This is why I didn't stick up for Sally when he told me that she had been too old for him. That he was going out with an eighteen-year-old now. Apparently they have a really strong connection and she interests him in a way Sally never really could. 'You know what they say about younger chicks,' he laughed, and then he asked me why I rang. I said I couldn't remember.

Afterwards I told Brian what Colin had said. I thought he might stick up for him, but he was disgusted.

'I guess that proves that some men are just genetically programmed to be jerks,' he said, and he put his arm around me. He didn't even try to squeeze my waist like he normally does.

Another interesting thing is that I remember Brian celebrating his fiftieth birthday last year.

See *Danger, Old, Weight, X-rated*

Z

Zeitgeist

I'm finding it difficult to concentrate on reading anything substantial at the moment. All that happens is that I end up reading the same lines over and over again, watching the letters dance on the page rather than trying to take in the words.

To fill in the time, I've taken to doing the questionnaires in women's magazines. The strange thing is that they all seem to be about subjects I need the answers to. I have learnt so much about myself as a result. I fill in those little crosses with as much concentration as my father used to tick off items on his list of things to do. My only worry is that I am slipping further and further down the age categories. I have noticed that in some magazines there are no boxes to tick if you are over the age of thirty-four. Presumably by this stage you will be too busy being successful to fill in questionnaires, but what happens if you don't manage that? How will you get to know things about yourself then?

See *Happiness, Illness, Impostor Syndrome, Routines, Teaching*

Zen

I can't remember how old I was when I realised that most things are better as memories than the real thing.

It's the same with photographs. Everybody always smiles for the camera so when you look back it is difficult to imagine a more glorious time. This is why when people are looking through a pile of photographs and suddenly stop to look at one a bit harder you know that it will be a picture of them. They are trying to remember what it felt like to be that happy and whether that moment was really more joyful than the – unrecorded, unremembered – present moment.

See *Ants, Impostor Syndrome, Kindness, Mars Bars, Noddy, Velvet, Woolworth's*

Zero

It's hard to pinpoint the exact time when work really did become something more than just a shield from the pain about John, but for the most part, it really is what I'm interested in nowadays.

There are even some days I can get through without crying.

I went to my first meeting as Brian's assistant the other day. The client said he was very impressed with our teamwork.

Brian took me out for a drink afterwards and told me I was a natural. He then told me exactly how he was feeling and what he was going through. It took a long time, but it was just nice to be sitting in a pub with someone who wasn't looking over their shoulder the whole time, or at their watch wondering whether they had enough time to take you home. Or not.

'I needed a wake-up call,' Brian said, 'and speaking of which, what are you like in the morning?' As we left, Brian whispered: 'We don't need to tell anyone at work about this, do we, Ver?' He kept calling me his little secret.

When Brian hugged me, it felt all wrong. I kept looking for spots to rest my head that just weren't there. His chin was bristly against my cheek, and I nearly passed out with how homesick I felt for John.

Brian's right about something though. Sometimes you just have to keep moving forward. I rang the solicitor again when I got home. He said I should feel happy to contact him, night or day.

See *Impostor Syndrome, Phantom E-mails, Teaching, Victim, Youth, Zen*

Zest

James, the solicitor, and I are opening the first of our broken-hearted hostels in six months' time. It's in my parents' old house, which is why we're calling it Rose's House. I think my mother would have liked that. The first of a bouquet of flowers, we hope.

It's like my life has started all over again. James says that with his experience and gravitas combined with my youth and energy we make a perfect partnership. He loves listening to my stories. We've got very close during the planning stages, although I've been careful not to let the relationship go beyond business at the moment.

'I've learnt the hard way,' I tell him, 'not to take anything for granted.'

We've agreed that all the money I've invested in our broken-hearted home scheme should be transferred into his name so he can handle the finances, leaving me free to concentrate on the creative planning and ideas. He's finally agreed that it's much better we both do what we're best at. Now he's got to know me better, he's more trusting in our relationship.

It was worth the effort. James makes me feel completely protected. It is so wonderful not to have to worry about anything at all. For the first time in my life, I'm pleased to be me.

See *Daisies, Doors, Houses, Money – Even More of It, New Men, True Romance, Yellow*

Zoology

Q: Why did the first monkey fall out of the tree?
A: Because it was dead.
Q: Why did the second monkey fall out of the tree?

A: Because it was holding the first monkey's hand.
Q: Why did the third monkey fall out of the tree?
A: Because it thought it was a game.

See *Captains, Danger, Influences, Ultimatum, Why?*

Zzzz

I woke up in the night realising that the poets I read when I was a teenager had got it wrong.

Love's not like a rollercoaster because of the ups and downs. It is more because you queue for hours to get on the ride, then you are strapped in so you can't get out even when you're about a third of the way through and realise you've changed your mind. There's nothing you can do, you've just got to carry on until the end and even then you've got to wait until someone else releases you and says you can go.

And once you're safely back on solid ground, you're rushing off to join the next queue.

Luckily I went back to sleep and by the time the alarm went off, I'd come to my senses and forgotten all about this.

I only remembered when Sally told me that she feels now that living with Colin made her feel she was strapped to a chair watching her life go by. I didn't tell her my theory. She'd only have related it to the solicitor or something silly like that.

Sally's going to be my date at the opening party for our hostel. She laughed when I told her that I wanted one room to be just like her parents' spare room, but after all, that was where I used to imagine myself when I was suffering the most after John. I haven't told Sally how I've kept that velvet scrap in my pocket the whole time. It's nearly worn out now.

Sally said she always wanted to live in my house. She said she used to secretly pretend my mother was hers.

It made me think. I want each room in my hostel to be decorated like a different dream of home. After all, home is like love. It's just a state of mind, a fantasy, that you can learn to live without if necessary.

I'm not going to invite anyone else to the party. Just Sally.

Reading Index

Animals
: *Ants – Blackbirds, Robins and Nightingales – Dogs – Elephant's Egg – Indecent Exposure – Revenge – Tornados – Vacuuming – Zoology*

Body
: *Blood – Breasts – Ears – Foreheads – Glenda G-Spot – Hair – Indecent Exposure – Mirrors – Moustache – Nostrils – Rochester – Startrite Sandals – Thrush – Visible – Weight – Withdrawal – Wrists*

Colin
: *Best Friends – Colin – Foreheads – Jealousy – Love Calculators – Rochester – Sculpture – Sex – Ultimatum – Why? – X-rated – X-ray Vision – Yard – Youth*

Deceit
: *Dreams – Elephant's Egg – Engagement Ring – Horoscopes – Lesbians – Mars Bars – Memory – Mistaken Identity – Money – Even More of It – Mystery Tours – Nursing – Old – Phantom E-mails – The Queen II – Utopia – Withdrawal*

Entrepreneurs
: *Ambition – Best Friends – Firefighting – Kisses – Money – Even More of It – Objects – Promotion – Ultimatum – Yields – Zest*

Fathers
: *Ambition – Ants – Houses – Illness – Lust – Mistaken Identity – Orphans – Outcast – Poverty – Routines – Thomas the Tank Engine – True Romance – Voices – Women's Laughter – Xenophobia*

Gastronomic
: *Baked Beans – Crème Caramel – Elephant's Egg – Ice Cream – Liqueur Chocolates – Mars Bars – Oranges*

Homes
: *Doors – Houses – Magazines – Noddy – Objects – Property – True Romance – Utopia – Velvet – Yellow*

Image
: *Boxing – Breasts – Codes – Danger – Fashion – Glitter – Gwyneth Paltrow – Happiness – Indecent Exposure – Mirrors – Moustache – New Men – Normals – Old – Outcast – The Queen – Startrite Sandals – Underwear – Visible – Voyeur – Weight – Wrists*

John	*See every entry in the alphabet*
Kate	*Kate – Lesbians – Letters – Old – Reasons – Stalking*
Lust	*Breasts – Fat Women – Ice Cream – Indecent Exposure – Jacuzzi – Kisses – Marathons – Objects – Phone Calls – Rude – Stationery – Thomas the Tank Engine – Toys – Vexed – Voyeur – Wrists*
Mothers	*Daisies – Elephant's Egg – Engagement Ring – Heroines – Houses – Illness – Influences – Mirrors – Mistaken Identity – Positive Thinking – Quick – Stepmothers – True Romance – Underwear – Velvet – Voices – Withdrawal – Women's Laughter – X – Zest*
Names	*Daisies – Glenda G-Spot – Names – Normals – Surnames – Words – You*
Outsiders	*Ants – Captains – Daisies – Fat Women – Mistaken Identity – Money – Noddy – Outcast – The Queen – Revenge – Stalking – Unfit – Vendetta – Voyeur – Washing Powder – Withdrawal – X*
Personal Development	*Ambition – Boxing – Dreams – Endings – God – Happiness – Heroines – Horror Movies – Impostor Syndrome – Kindness – Omens – Pain Index – Positive Thinking – Teaching – Weight – Wobbling – X – Zeitgeist*
Relations	*Baked Beans – Blood – Daisies – Danger – Elephant's Egg – Illness – Mirrors – Mistaken Identity – Only Children – Orphans – Relatives – Stepmothers – Underwear – Zzzz*
School	*Blackbirds, Robins and Nightingales – Blood – Captains – The Fens – Mars Bars – Outcast – Telephone Boxes – Woolworth's*
Telephones	*Marathons – Phone Calls – Surnames – Telephone Boxes – Washing Powder – Women's Laughter – X-rated – Yard – Yields – Youth – Zero – Zest*
Unfairness	*Ants – Baked Beans – Blackbirds, Robins and Nightingales – Crème Caramel – Danger – Doors – God – Mystery Tours – Noddy – Quick – Thrush – Ultimatum – Vendetta – Victim – Why? – Withdrawal – Youth – Zoology*
Vengeance	*Ants – Dogs – Engagement Ring – Letters – Mistaken Identity – Nursing – Old – Revenge – Zest*
Women	*Ambition – Boxing – Breasts – Fat Women – Glenda G-Spot – Glitter – Gossip – Heroines – Lesbians – Moustache – Old – Sex – Stationery – Toys – Underwear – Voices – Weight – Withdrawal – Women's Laughter*

ACKNOWLEDGEMENTS

Grateful thanks to Anne Hay, Rob Middlehurst, Sheenagh Pugh, Jenny Newman and James Friel for generously passing on their knowledge and enthusiasm; to Alex Patterson and Esther Dermott for being the hardest act to follow; to Robert Doyle, Mo McAuley, Gaye Jee, Malcolm Lewis, Frank Dullaghan, Victor Tapner and Shaun Levin for supportive reading; to Lynne Rees for the title; to Rosemary Davidson and Victoria Millar for their valued expertise and support; to my agent Rupert Heath, without whom, and of course, to my family, always, for everything.

A NOTE ON THE TYPE

The text of this book is set in Linotype Stempel Garamond, a version of Garamond adapted and first used by the Stempel foundry in 1924. It's one of several versions of Garamond based on the designs of Claude Garamond. It is thought that Garamond based his font on Bembo, cut in 1495 by Francesco Griffo in collaboration with the Italian printer Aldus Manutius. Garamond types were first used in books printed in Paris around 1532. Many of the present-day versions of this type are based on the *Typi Academiae* of Jean Jannon cut in Sedan in 1615.

Claude Garamond was born in Paris in 1480. He learned how to cut type from his father and by the age of fifteen he was able to fashion steel punches the size of a pica with great precision. At the age of sixty he was commissioned by King Francis I to design a Greek alphabet, for this he was given the honourable title of royal type founder. He died in 1561.